DE

"The lady's with me," Fargo said to the man who was manhandling the saloon girl, Lucia.

"Have it your way," the man said, pushing her roughly toward him. Fargo helped her up from the floor and was heading back to his table when he heard the soft whisper of a pistol drawn from a holster.

Fargo pushed Lucia to one side and dived in the opposite direction as a gunshot split the air. He crashed in the middle of a card game, and rolled away instantly as the table collapsed under him. He came up on his feet, Colt in hand.

The man stood ten feet away, pistol drawn, eyes black slits.

"Where I come from, we don't shoot men in the back," Fargo said.

The gunman's answer came quick. "In Deadwood, we shoot 'em any way we can."

AMERICAN VOICES

☐ **THE JUNGLE by Upton Sinclair.** In some of the most harrowing scenes ever written in modern literature, Upton Sinclair vividly depicted factory life in Chicago in the first years of the twentieth century.

(524209—$2.95)

☐ **ARROWSMITH.** Afterword by Mark Schorer. The story of Martin Arrowsmith and his devotion to science which ultimately isolates him as a seeker after truth. A portrait of the American whose work becomes his life. (522257—$5.95)

☐ **O PIONEERS! by Willa Cather.** The author's second novel in which she creates the first of her memorable, strong heroines. Alexandra Bergson inherits her father's failing farm, raises her brothers alone, and is torn by the emergence of an unexpected passion. A literary landmark, with an introduction by Elizabeth Janeway. (522850—$4.50)

☐ **THE SONG OF THE LARK by Willa Cather.** Thea Kronberg is a fiesty girl whose upbringing in a raw, provincial Colorado town nearly stifles her artistic ambitions. Here is a wonderful portrait of a young woman who makes her own destiny. (525337—$4.95)

☐ **WINESBURG, OHIO by Sherwood Anderson.** The mixed Sherwood Anderson's memories of his boyhood in Clyde, Ohio and his observations in turn-of-the-century Chicago. A modern American classic that embraces frankness and truth, and deals with people whose deeply moving lives are filled with secrets. (525698—$4.95)

Price slightly higher in Canada.

THE
TRAILSMAN
136

TEXAS
TRIGGERS

by

Jon Sharpe

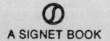

A SIGNET BOOK

SIGNET
Published by the Penguin Group
Penguin Books USA Inc., 375 Hudson Street,
New York, New York 10014, U.S.A.
Penguin Books Ltd, 27 Wrights Lane,
London W8 5TZ, England
Penguin Books Australia Ltd, Ringwood,
Victoria, Australia
Penguin Books Canada Ltd, 10 Alcorn Avenue,
Toronto, Ontario, Canada M4V 3B2
Penguin Books (N.Z.) Ltd, 182-190 Wairau Road,
Auckland 10, New Zealand

Penguin Books Ltd, Registered Offices:
Harmondsworth, Middlesex, England

First published by Signet,
an imprint of New American Library,
a division of Penguin Books USA Inc.

First Printing, April, 1993
10 9 8 7 6 5 4 3 2 1

The first chapter of this book originally appeared in *Montana Mayhem*,
the one hundred thirty-fifth volume in this series.

 REGISTERED TRADEMARK—MARCA REGISTRADA

Printed in the United States of America

The Trailsman

Beginnings . . . they bend the tree and they mark the man. Skye Fargo was born when he was eighteen. Terror was his midwife, vengeance his first cry. Killing spawned Skye Fargo, ruthless, cold-blooded murder. Out of the acrid smoke of gunpowder still hanging in the air, he rose, cried out a promise never forgotten.

The Trailsman they began to call him all across the West: searcher, scout, hunter, the man who could see where others only looked, his skills for hire but not his soul, the man who lived each day to the fullest, yet trailed each tomorrow. Skye Fargo, the Trailsman, the seeker who could take the wildness of a land and the wanting of a woman and make them his own.

1860, Texas—
on the edge of the Circle T Ranch,
a town called Deadwood,
where broken men
lived or died by their trigger fingers
and a man's word was the only law . . .

1

A lonely sound. The goddamn loneliest sound in the world, he thought. The rhythmic creak of rope against the branch of a cottonwood tree carried faintly on the dry wind.

The pinto under him heard it too and shifted nervously, nostrils flaring. The horse shook its head and nickered low. The smell of blood always made it shy like that, he thought, narrowing his lake blue eyes.

Skye Fargo turned his gaze from the solitary tree in the distance and surveyed the gray chaparral that spread out around him in all directions. The thickets were pale green in places, beginning to bud in the early spring warmth. The land was broad and seemingly endless, crinkling off to the south into a gulch and probably a river, he thought, noting the darker band of low land. Ahead he saw short hills. The sun blazed overhead in the pale blue sky which faded to white at the distant horizon. There was no one in sight. Whoever had done it had come and gone without waiting to see if the job was finished.

Frontier justice was swift, he thought, as he put his spur to the Ovaro and rode down the long slope toward the four men swinging from the cottonwood—swift and sometimes dead wrong.

One of the men was still kicking, as if running

from death. He dangled above the ground, his legs pumping in a hopeless struggle for breath as the knotted rope slowly strangled him. A hanged man was lucky if his neck broke immediately, Fargo thought, looking at the three still bodies hanging heavily from the tree. As he galloped nearer, he saw that the four had been shot too. Blood darkened the front of their shirts. That was the scent the wind had carried to the Ovaro's sensitive nostrils. Fargo arrived just as the man's battle ended. The flailing legs suddenly lost power, twitched once, and were still.

Fargo sat on his pinto, observing the four men hanging before him, heads bent toward their shoulders, faces dark, hands tied behind their backs. The ropes groaned as the wind caught the bodies and swung them back and forth. A hawk wheeled high overhead. The vultures would arrive soon.

He wondered who the men were. Horse thieves, murderers, bandits, maybe. But as he studied the men's clothing, he doubted it. They looked like ordinary cowpunchers, with their weather-stained chaps, rope-hardened hands, and wide-brimmed hats. And they were just boys, younger than twenty, he guessed. One was tow-headed, one carrot-topped, and two dark, maybe Mexican. Now why would four young punchers get hanged in the middle of nowhere in Texas? Maybe they were part of a gang of rustlers.

It would be prudent to find out who they were, Fargo thought. If he could. He didn't know this part of southern Texas, but if somebody was out on a hanging spree, it would be a good idea to find out as much as possible.

Fargo drew his Colt and fired in rapid succession at the four ropes. The bodies fell heavily, one by one, onto the hard-packed dry earth. Fargo dismounted.

The redhead had nothing in his pockets but a well-fingered tintype of a saloon girl with one leg on a chair and her garters showing. Fargo replaced it in the boy's pocket.

One of the Mexican boys lay on his side and, as Fargo turned the body face-up, the boy groaned faintly. Fargo loosened the rope around his neck; it was high around his ear, saving the boy from strangulation. But the bullet wound in his chest had hit just below the breastbone. Blood was flowing fast; he wouldn't last long, Fargo realized. And there was every possibility he shouldn't. For all he knew, the boy was a thief and was hanged justly. But somehow he found himself doubting it.

The boy's lids fluttered open and his eyes, dark and soft brown, focused slowly on Fargo's face. The boy's lips moved slightly. He was trying to talk. Well, at least that would tell him something, Fargo thought.

Fargo fetched his canteen and splashed a few drops of water on the boy's lips. He could see the struggle on the boy's face as he tried to form words but failed. The sun beat down, and Fargo felt the sweat drip from under his hat. He moved so that he shaded the boy from the sun's glare. After a moment the boy tried again and the words came slowly.

"Take . . . message to . . . Il Patrone," the boy said in a heavy accent. Fargo nodded encouragement. "Please . . . take message or many more . . . many more will die." The boy paused and swallowed dry. Fargo splashed a little more water on his lips. A drink would only choke the boy now, and it wouldn't save his life. The boy's eyes shone with gratitude for the water. "Please . . . promise," he muttered. "Promise . . ." The boy paused expectantly, his eyes begging Fargo for a reply.

"Promise," Fargo repeated, before he knew what he was doing.

Relief washed over the boy's face. "Promise," he repeated in a thick accent. "Tell Il Patrone. Only Il Patrone and no one else. No other person." He paused with the effort. "Tell Il Patrone that . . ." the voice weakened to barely a whisper. ". . . that team works for the sheriff. Team is against Il Patrone now." Fargo puzzled over the words, not sure if he had heard right.

"The team works for the sheriff?" Fargo repeated. "The team is against Il Patrone?"

The boy's gaze clouded with frustration, and he looked as if he might speak again, but his eyes suddenly went dull and the mouth sagged open. Fargo eased the boy to the ground and went through his pockets.

Fargo found only knives, bits of jerky, and the one photograph on the boys, nothing that would shed light on who they were and why they were hanged. He laid the bodies out side by side and considered burying them. If they were thieves, they should be left to the vultures. But if they were innocent, they deserved a burial. Since he didn't know, he decided to leave them as they were. He remounted the pinto and rode west again in the direction he'd been heading, thinking about the boy's last words.

Fargo had been looking forward to a leisurely trip across Texas to New Orleans, where he'd been planning a month of relaxation. The image of a dark-haired Creole woman with a slender waist floated up before him, and for a moment he felt the pull of her. He should forget the hanging incident and ride on.

But Fargo had given his promise. The boy had died believing that the stranger who leaned over him would deliver his message to Il Patrone, whoever the hell that was. And, according to the kid, the team was on the side of the sheriff. If he delivered the message, would he be helping the wrong side, Fargo wondered.

The boy's voice still echoed in his ears, "Take message or many more die." The question was, if he found Il Patrone and delivered the boy's message, would it save the lives of thieves? Or of innocent people?

A mile farther Skye spotted a saddled horse grazing alone. He galloped over, prepared to rope it. But it did not move at his approach. He slowed, leaned out from his pinto, and caught up the reins of the docile chestnut, pulling her alongside.

The saddle was spattered with blood, a dark stain on the leather-covered horn and the front of the seat. It was nearly new, the leather still pale honey and, except for the blood, unstained. Fargo noted the heads of longhorn steers tooled on the fenders that hung down on either side. He examined the stamp of the Kansas City maker on the corner of the skirt. His eye was caught by a brand on the chestnut's haunch—T enclosed by an O. Brands were always read from the outside in. The Circle T, Fargo thought to himself.

He'd heard of the Circle T Ranch, reputed to be the biggest spread in Texas. But its size was all he knew about it. No doubt the chestnut had belonged to one of the four dead boys. So they had come from the Circle T . . . unless they had stolen the mount. But in that case, whoever hanged them would have caught the horse and taken it back to the ranch. None of it made sense. Maybe he would meet someone who could enlighten him, he thought as he tied the horse behind him and rode on.

DEADWOOD, TEXAS, the tilted sign read. LEAVE YOUR GUN IN YOUR HOLSTER. POPULATION . . . Beneath the last line were several figures. One hundred seventy-three had been scratched out as had one hundred forty-nine and several more numbers. The final figure written was eighty-four, but someone had marked through that as well and not bothered to add another.

A well stood in the middle of the wide dusty street, or rather in the middle of the space between the buildings, since there were hardly enough of them to define a street. A few board shacks were scattered along one side. An imposing gallows of weathered gray board crooked a tall finger against the sky. From it swung two empty nooses. A moving figure caught Fargo's eye and he reined in.

A man dragging a body disappeared between two of the shacks. At the other end of the street Fargo saw a second body lying in the dust. Even at a distance Fargo's keen eyesight could make out the silver pistol still in the hand of the outflung arm, the natty clothing of the professional gunslinger, and the blood pooling darkly to one side of the body. All was silent. Still.

A big mud-brick building with barred windows and a pointed tin roof sported a sign reading COUNTY BANK, ALL DEPOSITS WELCOME. Across the way was a corral, stable, and a few more board shacks. Fargo heard a sound and moved forward. In a side yard a man who was hammering a coffin didn't look up as Fargo clopped down the street. No one else was in sight.

Fargo saw a tall false-fronted building with bat-wing doors that had a few horses tethered outside. He headed for it, wondering who had been in the shoot-out. Maybe someone in the saloon would know who Il Patrone was and what the hangings were all about.

Fargo pushed inside the doors and entered the murky room. As his eyes adjusted to the dimness, he heard the sound of sudden movement, of men pushing their chairs away from the tables and of guns being cocked. Squinting in the gloom he paused and surveyed the saloon. A dozen men had hunkered down around the room, all with their attention on him. Half had ducked behind tables, and several had their pistols drawn and cocked.

"Expecting somebody?" Fargo said with a grin. He slowly moved his hands out from his hips to show he had no intention of drawing. Nobody moved.

"What d'ye want, stranger?" a thick voice asked. Fargo located the speaker standing by the bar, a black-bearded man with a pot belly. He held an Allen and Thurber Dragoon in front of him, a model from the gold rush days. They weren't accurate, but the old '49ers could make a nasty hole at close range, Fargo thought, looking down the broad barrel.

"Passing through. Just stopped for a friendly drink," Fargo answered, his voice not at all friendly. Some welcome to Deadwood.

Fargo raised his hands slightly, further from his Colt. His tall muscular frame was tense, ears alert, ready to draw at any sudden motion from the men. After a long moment the man at the bar relaxed and holstered his pistol. The rest of the men did as well, returning to their chairs.

"Never can be too sure," the man mumbled. Fargo walked further into the saloon, or what passed for one in Deadwood, Texas, and joined the black-bearded man at the bar. The man didn't look at him, and Fargo turned to survey the room.

Five rickety tables and a bunch of mismatched chairs filled the small dark chamber. The men, dressed in dusty clothes and weather-beaten hats, hunched over card games. One wall was covered, floor to ceiling, with sun-bleached skulls—buffalo, antelope, armadillo, cougar, badger, even a couple of human ones, all jumbled together.

As Fargo turned back, a skinny bartender poked his head above the counter. "Help you?" he asked, eyes darting nervously.

"What's the local brew?" Fargo asked.

"Red-eye."

"Some of that," Fargo said. He watched as the man poured two fingers into a shot glass and slid it across the bar. Just as Fargo raised it to his mouth, a second figure appeared from behind the counter.

The woman was plump in all the right places, dark-eyed and dark-haired, probably from across the border, he thought. She pulled her shawl close about her and caught his eye. He smiled encouragingly. She looked away, and he tipped up the glass.

"Had a shoot-out?" Fargo asked the black-bearded man standing next to him.

After a minute the man grunted assent.

"Who was it?" Fargo asked, idly rolling the empty glass between his fingers.

The man shrugged. Another moment passed. The bartender noticed Fargo's glass was empty and re-filled it.

"You got a helluva lot of questions, stranger," the man muttered.

It was Fargo's turn to shrug, and he did.

"We get a lot of gunslingers coming through," the man added. "Can't keep track of 'em all."

"Where's the sheriff?" Fargo asked.

The man shrugged again. "Out," he said. Another minute passed, and Fargo assumed the conversation was over.

"Riding around," the man added at last.

If he expected answers from this man, he'd be waiting forever, Fargo realized. He turned his attention toward the girl.

"Well?" the bartender whispered, nudging her. "Get over there." She flicked the bartender an angry look and came around the bar, sidling up to Fargo, who swallowed the second drink.

Red-eye was well named, Fargo thought, his eyes watering slightly from the fire of the brew. A few of the men left the bar. Others were engrossed in serious card playing and drinking. The black-bearded man joined one of the games. Fargo glanced down at the woman at his elbow.

"My name is Lucia," she said, almost in a whisper, her Spanish accent unmistakable. "What's yours?"

"Skye Fargo," he answered with a nod.

"Nice name," she said, blinking her long, dark lashes. Her eyes glanced at the empty glass. "Another?"

Before he answered or even nodded, the bartender reached for the shot glass and refilled it hastily. So that was the game, Fargo thought, his eyes lingering on her low neckline. She'd get the customers drunk, then take them up the back stairs. Or rob them. Or worse. He'd seen the game before.

17

Fargo wrapped his large fist around the shot glass but kept it on the countertop.

"Where're you from?" he asked.

Her dark brows shot up. "Me? From?" Lucia looked surprised to be asked a question. "Piedritas," she answered. "Across the border."

The bartender had begun to dry glasses, humming to himself, but clearly listening to every word.

"What are you doing up here?" Fargo asked, still not taking a drink. She was damn pretty and very young. Too much of both to be stuck in this town.

Lucia smiled up at him, responding to his interest. "I was looking for my sister. And this is as far as I got when I ran out of money. My sister's name is Angelina." He smiled at her, nodding. Then her words came out in a rush, as if they'd been dammed up for a long time and had needed release. "Maybe you have seen her. She looks like me, Angelina. But she is older—"

The bartender, his back turned to them, rapped a glass on the bar, a clear signal she wasn't doing her job. Lucia looked flustered for an instant.

"But . . . but what about you?" she asked, looking up and blinking her eyes at him again.

Poor kid, he thought. She ran out of money in Deadwood, Texas. What luck. He smiled at her but didn't answer.

"Please, drink." She gestured toward the redeye.

"I'll switch to beer," Fargo said. He wanted to keep his wits about him. But it would be pleasant to have some female company for a couple of hours. And maybe he could find out something from her more easily than from the men. He tossed coins down on the counter and took the two beers the bartender poured, leaving the shot of red-eye on the bar.

"Let's get over here," Fargo said, leading her to a just-vacated table under a sun-bleached buffalo skull with eye sockets the size of two fists. As he settled in, he noticed the bartender pick up the abandoned shot glass, shrug, and carefully pour the red-eye back into the bottle.

"So, what's this about your sister?" he asked, sliding her one of the beers.

She took it and smiled. "I heard she headed this direction . . . but you don't want to hear my troubles," she added, embarrassed.

"Then tell me about the shoot-out," he said, nodding toward the street. He would start with the obvious questions and see if he could get a sense of the place. Maybe she'd know something; maybe she wouldn't.

"Oh that," she said shrugging, as the man at the bar had. "There's a shoot-out every day, it seems."

"And the sheriff doesn't do anything about it?"

"Him!" She spit on the floor before she could stop herself, then looked down. "He's hardly ever in town anyway. There are big troubles on the ranch south of here."

"What kind of trouble?"

"Rustlers. It's the Spill brothers and their gang."

"I've heard of them," Fargo said. "They've been rustling for a long time."

"Yes," Lucia said, taking a swallow of the beer. "We know them in Mexico too. Anyway, the Spill brothers came through Deadwood awhile back. The sheriff caught them and locked them up. But the night before he was going to hang them, they escaped. They're out there somewhere, stealing longhorns from the big ranch."

"The Circle T?"

"Yes, that's the name."

"And the sheriff's gone to the ranch to help?"

"Not exactly. He and his posse have been patrolling the border of the Circle T," she said. Her eyes glittered as if she were happy to be telling him a secret. "There is something strange about that because everybody says he is not welcome on the ranch. The ranch hands don't like anybody to come onto the ranch, especially the sheriff."

"How can they stop him?"

"The Circle T has . . . riders. They call them . . ."

"Line riders?" Fargo guessed.

"Yes, that is the word. Line riders. These men ride all around the ranch to keep people out."

"And the cattle in," Fargo said.

"I suppose," she said doubtfully. "But they say if you go on the Circle T land, these riders will shoot you first. They keep to themselves on the Circle T."

"So, why is the sheriff helping them?"

Lucia grinned and pointed to a piece of paper tacked to one wall. Fargo rose and went to inspect it. On the wanted poster were the two crudely drawn faces of the Spill brothers. It read: WANTED, DEAD OR ALIVE: SPILL BROS. JAS. & THEO.— $1,000 REWARD FOR BOTH. $400 FOR ONE. He sat back down beside Lucia.

"That's a hefty reward."

"People say that the sheriff's mad as a hornet that the Spill brothers got away. They're impossible to catch," she said. "But I think the sheriff wants the money very much. Ever since they escaped, the sheriff's been out all the time trying to find them."

Fargo smiled at her and she smiled back, her round cheeks dimpling. His mind was in a whirl.

Maybe the four kids had been from the Spill brothers gang. But even as he thought this, he felt it was wrong. They just didn't look like rustlers. He'd try a more interesting question on her. "Ever hear of Il Patrone?" he asked.

"Il Patrone?" she repeated, her eyes thoughtful. "It means The Patron in your language." She thought a moment and then shook her head. "No, it does not mean anything to me. But it is a title of great honor in my country. Only great men are called Il Patrone."

Fargo nodded and took a swallow of beer. "Any great men around here?" he said, looking furtively toward the dusty men playing cards.

She giggled and then grew serious. "Well, there is Mr. Owen Tate," she said.

"Who's that?" Fargo asked.

"He owns the Circle T," Lucia answered. "He is the most powerful man in Texas. Maybe in the whole country. But I hear he is a very bad man, very dangerous."

"Dangerous?" he repeated. "How so?"

"Well, I don't know," she said slowly. "That is what people say. I guess he is so powerful that, on his ranch, everyone does what he says. His word is the law."

"That could be dangerous," Fargo agreed, thinking of the four dead boys. "What does he look like?"

Lucia laughed. "No one ever sees Mr. Owen Tate! Even his men do not come into Deadwood. They always stay on the ranch. I hear the Circle T is so big a man can ride for three days and hardly make it across."

Fargo nodded. He had heard that too. The idea of all that land belonging to one man was staggering. With enough men like Owen Tate there wouldn't be any free room on the plains. He shook his head slowly at the thought and set his empty glass on the table.

"I'll get us another round," Lucia said, rising. A rangy fellow entered the doors and approached the bar at the same moment she did. The man removed his hat and combed lanks of greasy hair back from his sweating face. Then he rubbed his hand down his shirt.

"Hot out," he grumbled to no one in particular.

Lucia stood waiting to get the beers. The man looked down at her, then reached over and put his hand on her rear. She stepped out of his reach.

"Whattsa matter?" he said to her. "Gimme a double shot," he added over his shoulder.

The bartender left the beers and hastened to do his bidding. Meanwhile the man grabbed Lucia around the waist and drew her close. She struggled. "Let me go," she said. "I am busy now. Later."

Fargo pushed his chair back noisily and slowly rose to his full height. The man looked up from Lucia, his eyes squinting as if taking Fargo's measure.

"The lady's with me at the moment," Fargo said.

One corner of the man's mouth twitched, then slowly raised in a half smile. "I don't feel like waiting," the man said. He pulled her closer and grabbed one of her breasts with his free hand. "This little woman's gonna give me what I want when I want it."

She pushed him away firmly and turned again to the bar. The man grabbed her arm, hard, and pulled her back toward him.

"I think the lady should make up her own mind," Fargo said.

"Have it your own way," the man said, pushing her roughly toward him. Lucia fell to the floor, and the man turned away, toward the bar. Fargo stepped forward and gave her a hand up. He had just headed back toward the table when he heard the unmistakable soft whisper of a pistol drawn from a leather holster.

He pushed Lucia off to one side and dived in the opposite direction as the crack of the gunshot split the air where he had been standing. Fargo landed in the middle of a card game and rolled away instantly as the table collapsed under him. He came up on his feet, Colt in hand. All around him men ducked for cover.

The man stood ten feet from him, pistol drawn, eyes narrowed to black slits. Fargo noted that he held his gun expertly, firm in the palm, low down by the hip. The man would be a good shot and had very nearly shot him in the back with no warning. Still, he was reluctant to gun a man down over bad manners.

"Where I come from, we don't shoot men in the back," Fargo said, his voice low.

"In Deadwood, we shoot 'em any way we can," the man answered. Fargo waited a moment, considering the situation.

"Walk out of here now, and we'll call it quits," Fargo said calmly, his finger firm on the trigger. The man looked at him for a long moment, and the corner of his mouth twitched again, very slightly, then curled up in a half smile.

"Sure," the man said. "Sure." He lowered his gun and Fargo did likewise, both of them slowly holstering them as they kept their eyes locked on each other. But before the man had completely holstered his pistol, he drew again in a flash. Fargo

23

was ready. He crouched to one side, pulled up his Colt, and fired. The gun exploded, the shot catching the man in the chest, and he spun almost all the way around before he slumped onto the floor.

Fargo felt a hot burn along one shoulder as he tumbled onto the wooden planked floor. He rolled once and came to his feet, advancing on the fallen figure.

Fargo kicked the gun out of the man's hand as he lay blank-faced, staring up at the pressed tin ceiling. The wound in his chest spurted blood, which made a bright red pool beside the body. There was silence in the saloon.

"Goddamn," the bartender said, rising up on his toes to look over the counter at the dead man. "Goddamn," he repeated, his face ashen. "You are in real trouble, stranger. You just shot the sheriff's chief deputy. He's gonna be pissed. Real pissed."

2

Fargo looked down at the dead man sprawled on the floor in front of him. He pushed back the edge of the man's vest with the pointed toe of his boot. Underneath a tarnished deputy's star was pinned to the shirt. Some lawman.

The burning on his shoulder drew his attention, and he cupped his hand over the wound where the deputy's bullet had grazed him. It wasn't very deep, he realized, but there was plenty of blood. It would clot soon.

"You're hurt!" Lucia said, coming up to stand next to him.

"Just a scratch," Fargo answered. He turned to the bartender. "The deputy shot first," he said. "Twice."

The bartender shrugged. "I . . . I didn't really see anything," the bartender said. "I was ducked down here behind the bar."

Fargo turned to the men now emerging from behind the overturned tables. "How about the rest of you?" he asked. "You saw what happened here. The deputy tried to shoot me in the back. Then he fired on me again."

The men didn't look at him, but righted their chairs and sat down again.

"How about you?" Fargo said, walking over to

stand in front of the black-bearded man, who was gathering together a scattered deck of cards. "Did you see what happened?"

"Sure," he said, not looking at Fargo. "Stranger came in. Shot the deputy. That's all I know." Fargo felt his anger mount.

Lucia rushed forward. "Lies!" she screamed. "That's not what happened, and you know it!" She grabbed the man's collar with both hands and tried to shake him, repeating the words over and over. The man removed her hands impatiently and waved her away. Fargo pulled her toward him. "Well, I saw what happened!" she said. "I'll tell the sheriff."

"Like the sheriff is going to believe a Mexican," one of the men muttered. "And a girl."

"The sheriff is awful fond of hanging," the black-bearded man said nonchalantly, starting to shuffle the cards.

Fargo returned to the bar. "You got a judge around here?" he asked the bartender.

"Circuit judge just came through a week ago," the bartender replied. "Strung up two horse thieves, Johnny Ole and Terry Mac. But he let off Pappy Macon. Judge ain't coming round again for another six months. At least." He dropped his voice. "Sheriff probably won't wait that long. Won't want you taking up room in the jail cell. He loves to hang folks. Why . . ."

While the bartender rattled on, Fargo thought fast. It wouldn't help him to run from Deadwood. That would make him look guilty of murder. On the other hand waiting around for the sheriff to return didn't sound too appealing either. If he could ride after the circuit judge and explain matters, he might at least get a fair trial. Hell, it was his best chance of clearing this up.

"Where was the judge going from here?" Fargo cut in.

"Hmph? Headed east, I think," the bartender said, stroking his chin. "Toward Brownwater. That's the nearest town to here. East, on the other side of the Tate Ranch. Course, the judge'll have to go all the way around the top of the ranch, cause Owen Tate don't let nobody ride across his land, even a judge."

Fargo eyed the men in the saloon. None of them seemed the least bit interested in him at the moment. But would they let him ride out of town after shooting the deputy? Well, he'd have to try it. But he'd watch his back. The bartender took another bottle of whiskey to one of the tables. One of the men got heavily to his feet and dragged the deputy's body out the doors and onto the front porch, returning a moment later and sitting again at the table.

"I'm going to try to catch up with the judge and bring him back here," Fargo whispered to Lucia as she stood beside him. "If the sheriff asks which way I went, tell him you think I headed west."

Lucia nodded. Watching the men Fargo edged toward the door. No one moved or even looked up. The bartender glanced over toward him, expressionless, as he eased out of the batwing doors.

Outside the wide street of Deadwood was deserted. The deputy lay crumpled on one side of the wooden porch. Fargo noted that the body he had seen as he rode in had been removed from the street. The dark dampness of blood in the dirt showed where the gunslinger had fallen.

Fargo unhitched his pinto and the new chestnut. Damn it, he knew even less about the hangings and

Il Patrone than when he had ridden into Deadwood. And he'd collected a heap of trouble to boot.

He mounted, keeping an eye on the saloon door. Surely some of the men would come after him when they noticed he had gone. But all was still. He was about to spur the horse when he heard the crackle of gravel to one side of the saloon. Someone had come around the side, probably slipping out the back door of the building to snipe at him. Instinctively he crouched and drew. Lucia appeared. She hurried over as he returned the Colt to his holster.

"Please take me with you," she said, standing next to his pinto. "Anywhere is better than here."

"I've got to ride fast," he said. "It's going to be a rough trip to catch up with the judge before the sheriff returns and forms a posse to find me. And I'll be coming back to Deadwood anyway for the trial."

"I can ride fast," she pleaded. "Besides, I am the only one who will tell what really happened in there."

Fargo considered her words for a moment. It was true that taking her along would be protecting his only truthful witness. He could expect no defense from the men in the saloon.

"Please," she begged, her dark eyes troubled. "I can't stay here any longer."

"Come on," he said, gesturing toward the chestnut. She mounted nimbly, hiking her skirts up so that she didn't have to sit sidesaddle. Above her high, laced boots her legs were rounded and shapely. They started off, and Fargo was relieved to see the expert way she handled the reins and the chestnut.

Fargo kept looking behind him as they galloped out of town, expecting at any moment to see the men giving chase, or at least shooting after them. But Deadwood remained quiet, sleeping under the hot spring sun.

The Buckhorn Trail led west out of Deadwood, along the top of a ridge and parallel to the Nueces River, which ran a mile south. Fargo rode fast, eager to put miles between him and Deadwood and hoping to catch up with the judge as quickly as possible. The whole thing was damned inconvenient, he thought. But, as he replayed the scene in his mind, he realized there was nothing else he could have done. He couldn't have let the deputy harass Lucia. And then it had been shoot or be shot. No, he hadn't had a choice.

"Hell," he swore out loud, and the Ovaro pricked its ears at the sound of his voice. Fargo turned to see Lucia riding close behind him. She noticed his attention and waved. She rode well, obviously experienced on horseback. He turned forward again to survey the trail ahead.

His keen eyes swept across the broad land, washed white in the blazing sun of midafternoon. The chaparral looked desolate only to someone who couldn't read it, Fargo thought. He scanned the dark clumps of greasewood and the yellow rabbitbrush dotted among the greening sage. A mockingbird flashed white in the thicket. It perched, flicking its tail from side to side and singing some other bird's song as they passed. To the south, along the river, he spotted the distinctive dark ruffles of live oak and anaqua trees. On the other side of the Nueces River was Owen Tate's ranch, the Circle T.

The trail curved to the north, and they surprised a herd of gray mule deer crossing the track. The deer froze momentarily, their eyes wide, then like dry leaves scattering in the wind they bounded away weightlessly into the brush.

Fargo's trained eyes picked up signs that the land had had cattle driven across it. The grasses were worn away and half-moon hoofprints were engraved on some of the bald spots. He slowed to examine the markings. The last herd had been a big one, driven through the previous spring.

The Buckhorn Trail was now heading northeast, following the curving river. He had never ridden this trail before, but he knew that up ahead was the intersection with a branch of the Shawnee cattle trail. For almost twenty years men had driven cattle north up the Shawnee, which led through Dallas, crossed the Red River into Indian Territory, led up to the Arkansas River, and then to the markets of Kansas City or St. Louis.

Over the years Fargo had known a lot of cowboys. They rode a rough trail, full of danger. On a cattle drive there were a lot of spectacular ways a man could die—Indians, stampedes, quicksand, rattlesnakes, hail, and lightning storms.

But, he mused, the blasted thing was that most cowpunchers met death from something more mundane. On a quiet day a puncher's galloping horse might catch a hoof in a gopher hole, the leg would snap, and the hapless cowhand would be crushed by his own steed. Or a bull might step on a wasp's nest and, stung and enraged, would gouge the nearest cowpoke. Those and a thousand other stupid accidents were how most men died on a cattle drive.

But then there were hangings and shootings, he thought, and his eyes grew hard and his mouth tightened in a grim line. The four boys who had been hanged were now more than twenty miles back. He'd like to find out what happened there. And he had promised a dying kid that he'd deliver his message. But he had his own problems now, and they were more immediate.

The trail dipped into a draw where a narrow creek gurgled. Fargo reined in and dismounted, leading the sweating Ovaro among the rocks toward the water. Lucia dismounted behind him and brought the chestnut down.

Fargo refilled his canteen and handed it to Lucia. He knelt and splashed the dust off his face, then cupped his hands and brought the sun-warmed water up to his mouth. It tasted flat and dusty, but it was wet and he drank long. Lucia wiped her wet mouth with the back of her hand and refilled the canteen, handing it back to Fargo.

"You're a good rider," he said. "Where'd you learn?"

"My father had horses," she said, smiling at the compliment. "Outside of Piedritas. There were a lot of horses and cattle when I was a girl. But then came dry weather for a few years. All the horses and cattle of the village began to starve. Most of the livestock was sold to gringos and brought up north. Some of the people of Piedritas followed the cattle up north too."

"Is that when your sister left?"

"No," she said, her dark eyes sad. "The cattle and horses left long ago. My sister came north only last year. My mother and father died after she left and . . ." Her large eyes filled with tears.

"And so, since you were alone, you decided to set out and find her." Fargo finished her sentence.

Lucia nodded mutely, biting her lip.

He looked away, measuring the sun. Afternoon

was passing. They needed to ride hard to make some more distance before stopping for the night. The Buckhorn Trail followed the curve of the Nueces River leading due north. He had planned to follow the Buckhorn east across Texas. He remembered seeing the long lazy curve of the trail on the map. Eventually the trail swung east again as the river swung around.

But now they needed to go due east toward the town of Brownwater on the eastern border of the Circle T. That's where the judge had gone with a week's head start. Every step north was another step south they would have to travel later to get to Brownwater, he thought impatiently.

He thought about Deadwood. When the sheriff returned and heard the story, it would be a simple matter to track the two of them and figure out they'd gone east on the Buckhorn. No doubt the sheriff would get together a posse and a length of rope and pursue them, Fargo thought. Their only hope was to keep moving. Lucia was riding well. Still, he doubted she could stay in the saddle throughout the long night ahead.

There was another chance, he realized. To save time he could leave the trail, cross the Nueces, and cut across the open land. He gazed at the distant blue plain on the other side of the shallow river and wondered if Owen Tate owned that land too.

Lucia had told him that she had heard that the Circle T line riders would shoot anyone trying to cross into the Tate ranch, even the sheriff. It sounded like an exaggeration, and he wondered if the story were true.

If the ranch hands came after him, he felt confident the Ovaro could outrun any other horse. The only problem was Lucia and the chestnut, he thought, looking her over. She'd have to come along since he couldn't abandon her in the middle of the trail.

He decided to turn off the Buckhorn and ride down to the Nueces to have a look. Maybe they could cross and take their chances on the ranch. Somehow the risk of dodging a rancher's bullets was more appealing than being overtaken by a posse with a hangman's noose.

"Let's get going," he said to Lucia. "Down this way." They mounted and he led off, following the draw down toward the river.

The leaves on the live oaks glistened hot silver in the afternoon sun. Fargo followed a line of trees down to the water, finding a dappled patch of cool shade. Suddenly something moving in the wind caught his eye, and he reined in.

Before him stood a live oak, taller and older than the others, its long thick arms outspread. Its leaves were sparse and all on one side. The trunk was half-blackened, and the tree was dying—struck by lightning. But that was not what had caught his eye.

Dangling from two of the largest branches were the remains of three ropes. The ends, frayed like dry straw, danced in the wind, high above the ground. One of the ropes had cut into the branch, and some of the bark on the side had been worn away, as if that man had struggled.

"What is it?" Lucia asked, worry in her voice as she reined in beside him.

Fargo wordlessly pointed upward, his keen eyes already scanning the land nearby. No fresh graves. No cairns. But there had been three of them hanged. And, judging from the marks on the branch, it had been recent.

"What is that rope . . . ?" Lucia's voice trailed

off as she realized the answer to her question. Her eyes widened when she looked upward. Then she shivered and glanced about anxiously. "It's those cattle rustlers. The Spill brothers."

Fargo nodded silently, his sharp blue eyes searching the ground around them for any clues. He leaned out from his saddle and looked down. The dry dust was a mass of confused footprints and hoofprints. At least ten men, he guessed. Shod hooves and high-heeled boots. A thin trace of one man's sharp roweled spurs, worn low. Fresh prints, no more than a day old.

"I guess the sheriff caught up with some of them here," Lucia continued. "He's been hanging every one of the gang he catches. But he still hasn't caught James and Theodore. Those are the two brothers. He's desperate to get that reward."

Fargo nodded again, eyes still searching, remembering the wanted poster in the bar. Suddenly he dismounted and strode over toward a clump of greasewood. Fargo bent and grasped the end of a rope entangled in the brush. He jerked it several times until it came free.

He turned back toward Lucia, coiling it slowly as he walked toward the Ovaro.

"A *reata*!" she said.

"Yes, a lariat," he said. "And from the Circle T." He paused beside her horse and pointed to the small brand burned into the leather patch that flared one end of the lariat.

"Oh!" Lucia exclaimed. "So, the *ranch hands* must have hanged the rustlers."

Fargo shrugged. "There's no telling who was hanged," Fargo said. "This *reata* doesn't prove anything. It's just interesting." He mounted the Ovaro and led again toward the water, his mind whirling with questions and images of dangling ropes.

At the bank they paused to look at the Nueces. The water flowed between low bluffs, broad and spread out across sand bars and gravel beds. It would be an easy matter to ford the stream if they didn't hit quicksand. The rivers in south Texas were famous for the fine white sand that lay on the bottom and could half swallow a horse in a few minutes. Fargo eyed the river, finding a zigzag course across it that put the horse on gravel beds for most of the way.

He didn't like the idea of riding across the Circle T. Still, it would shorten their trip to the town of Brownwater and the circuit judge by at least a hundred miles. If they ran into the ranchers, he would talk their way through.

"Stay here," he instructed Lucia. "Let me try first. Then follow on my signal." She nodded, and he started the Ovaro across. The pinto, accustomed to fording rivers, had no trouble finding firm footing, and they emerged a minute later on the opposite bank. Fargo had just lifted his arm to signal Lucia when a shot rang out, followed by a shout. Fargo looked up to see a rider galloping down the hill toward him, rifle in hand. Lucia paused at the edge of the opposite bank.

"Hey you!" the rider shouted as he neared. "Where do you think you're going?" The ranch hand was young, like the four dead boys, and dressed in a puncher's chaps and broad hat.

"Howdy," Fargo said, raising his hand. "Are you from the Circle T Ranch?"

"You're on it," the kid said, his voice firm. He was brown-haired and heavily freckled. "Now I suggest you turn right around and get back off it."

"No harm meant," Fargo said. "I need to get to Brownwater as quick as I can. It's a matter of life and death. I was wondering if we could cut across this corner of the ranch. It would sure help us."

The kid looked him up and down slowly, then glanced across the river and started. Fargo followed his gaze. Lucia was nowhere to be seen.

"Where'd your partner go?" the puncher asked, clutching his rifle and nervously looking around. Fargo caught a glimpse of movement in the sagebrush across the river.

"She's just gone into the bushes. She's shy," he answered.

"She?" the kid repeated, glancing across again hopefully.

"Well, how about it?" Fargo asked. "Can we ride across the ranch? We're not troublemakers."

"Sorry," the ranch hand said after a long moment, his voice hardening. "Orders are orders. Mr. Tate doesn't allow strangers riding on the ranch anymore. Any strangers."

"Anymore?" Fargo asked. "Since when?"

"Since two months ago when the Spill brothers started making trouble. And . . . things started happening."

Fargo didn't like the way the kid said the word *things*. "What kind of things?"

The cowpuncher tightened his lips, and his pale blue eyes grew steely cold as he looked back at Fargo. "Just get going," he said brusquely, lowering the rifle a few inches for emphasis. The conversation was clearly over.

Fargo nodded and turned the pinto back around. He headed back across the river. He felt a slight twitch between his shoulder blades, and he wondered if the kid would shoot him in the back. He'd almost been killed once that way today, but he emerged safely on the opposite bank and turned back. The puncher was just where he had left him, watching. Fargo and the Ovaro plunged into the sage thicket.

"Lucia," he called out. She was behind him in a moment, and their two horses climbed through the underbrush up out of the river gully. As they rode, he repeated his conversation with the boy.

"I'm not surprised," said Lucia. I've heard they're serious about keeping people out."

When Fargo turned back, he could no longer see the kid, but he was sure, somehow, that he was still watching. "Let's cut back over the Buckhorn Trail," he said. "Looks like that's our best chance. We'll just ride hard as we can."

They galloped for a quarter hour over rough country before they hit the trail again and then followed the curving track that led northeast, following the river, the vegetation thinning to yellow grassland. They were starting up a long rise when Fargo heard hoofbeats ahead of them. He looked around. They couldn't be in a more exposed position, riding up a bare hillside.

He slowed the pinto, and Lucia came up next to him. There was no place to take cover. If they turned and galloped away, they would look suspicious to the riders cresting the hill. But if they continued on to meet them, they might just pass by.

"What is it?" Lucia pulled the chestnut up beside him.

"Riders ahead. Coming this way," he said, letting the Ovaro lope forward and touching the butt of his Colt.

Just then several mounted figures appeared, silhouetted against the late afternoon clouds. More appeared until there were two dozen men riding down the hill toward them. Fargo heard Lucia gasp.

"What is it?" he asked quietly.

"It's who. It's the sheriff and his men," she answered under her breath as the riders drew near.

3

The mounted men swarmed down the hill toward Fargo and Lucia. The Ovaro's ears pricked and he whinnied softly. Fargo touched his holstered Colt again and scanned the men. They were all armed.

Fargo thought fast. The sheriff and his men, riding back toward Deadwood, could not have heard about the shooting of the deputy. Maybe they would just ride by. But that was unlikely. Strangers passing on the trail usually stopped to exchange the news. Well, he would bluff his way by them, Fargo thought uneasily.

When they came within hailing distance, a sturdy-looking man raised his hand, and the posse drew up short. The sun glinted off the gold star on the man's vest. The sheriff, Fargo guessed. Fargo and Lucia reined in and sat on their horses opposite the sheriff and his men.

"What're you doing so far out of Deadwood, Miss Lucia?" the sheriff said at last, removing his hat. The sun caught the bright gold of his hair. "And who's this character?" The sheriff's voice was loud and commanding.

"My name's Skye Fargo," he answered for her. "Just passing through."

"I've heard of you. You're called the Trailsman," the sheriff said, conveying nothing with the tone of his voice. It always surprised Fargo how far his reputation had spread through the West. Fargo had heard some of the stories told about him. Some were true. Some had changed in the telling until he hardly recognized them. There was a silence, broken only by the creaking of saddles and the stamping of the horses.

Fargo measured the sheriff. He had grown accustomed to estimating men from the way they rode. The sheriff held the reins of his bay with one hand and kept them taut. He was tall, Fargo noted, broad-shouldered and muscular. His wavy bright blond hair glistened in the sun and emphasized the dark tan of his face. His green eyes were lightened by pale brows, bleached by the sun. And, even in the saddle, Fargo could see that the sheriff wore his gunbelt low and loose about his hips, as if he were careless and didn't need a gun. But the man was not careless, Fargo felt. He was coiled, wary, and ready. Yes, he was a man who would be a very efficient sheriff.

The sheriff's saddle was not new, but was well-soaped and glossy. His spurs and pistol shone silver, and his rifle gleamed black. Fargo noted a disc of highly polished metal hanging on one side of his saddle, and he wondered what it was for.

In the long silence the sheriff took a close look at him as well. Fargo's eyes flicked over the men, noting their pistols and rifles at the ready, their dusty clothes and tough, stringy horses. In the shade of their hat brims their eyes were dark and narrowed against the blinding brightness of the day. They seemed a tough bunch like the other men he had seen in Deadwood—quiet and wary. He'd hate to be on the wrong side of the law and facing this posse. A wry smile crossed Fargo's face as he realized he was in exactly that position. But luckily the posse didn't know it. Yet.

"And you must be the sheriff," Fargo said at last.

"Yep. Buck Witchell's the name," the man replied. "Now, why are you heading out of Deadwood with Miss Lucia?"

"I'm . . . I'm going to find my sister," Lucia cut in.

Witchell nodded thoughtfully. "You oughta be back in Deadwood, Miss Lucia," he muttered. "Working at the bar. I don't think they can manage that place without you."

Lucia shrugged.

"I have a right to go where I please," she answered.

Buck Witchell wiped his forehead with the back of his sleeve and put his hat back on. "I guess you do," he said slowly. "Still, I don't like the idea of you leaving Deadwood so all of a sudden. Doesn't seem right."

"It isn't sudden," she protested. "I've . . . I've been planning to move on for a while. I just never told anybody."

Buck Witchell nodded again, but the wariness remained in his eyes and in his coiled muscles.

Fargo was suddenly damned sorry he dragged the girl into this. Now that the sheriff had seen her with him, he might suspect she was involved in the shooting. He swore silently to himself.

"So," the sheriff said. "Where are you heading?"

"North up the Shawnee," Fargo answered for them. "To Dallas."

When the posse returned to Deadwood, he thought, they'd hear about his shooting the deputy, and they'd be back on the trail chasing him and Lucia. If the sheriff believed they had headed north up the Shawnee, it would give them another couple of hours lead before the posse figured out the ruse and doubled back. By then he and Lucia would be halfway to Brownwater, which lay east. Of course there was every possibility that the sheriff would figure Fargo had been lying about his destination. The sheriff looked like a man who was not easily fooled.

"It's almost time for the spring cattle drives," the sheriff remarked idly, sounding less suspicious. "Of course you're going to beat them all to Dallas."

"Yep," Fargo agreed. "I guess the Shawnee Trail must get crowded around this time of year."

"We're expecting the first drives through next week," Buck Witchell said. "They all come along the Buckhorn Trail and through Broken Promise Draw to get into the Shawnee."

Fargo nodded. The sheriff was beginning to sound downright friendly. Once again he wondered what the dying boy meant by his words, "Team works for the sheriff. Team is against Il Patrone now." Fargo felt the burden of promise, his promise to the dying boy to deliver his message only to Il Patrone and to no one else. Maybe the posse was the "team." They were certainly working for the sheriff. In that case Il Patrone might be on the wrong side of the law. But who the hell was Il Patrone? The sheriff would know.

"I heard there's somebody around here called Il Patrone," Fargo said. "Who is that?"

The sheriff's laugh was a short bark, painful to hear. There was pain in the laugh too, Fargo thought. Old pain—the kind of pain a man carries deep.

"Il Patrone," Buck repeated. "Ha! Why that's what Owen Tate's slaves call him. Patron. Ha!

Owen Tate is one of the crookedest, most dangerous men in Texas. He's been stealing land for almost twenty years now. His ranch slaves will shoot anybody who sets foot on his land. He's holed up in his big hacienda in the middle of the Circle T spread. Nobody can get near him. He's got more acres than any one man has a right to. And he's still trying to get more. He's trying to get control of all the land around here. Why, unless he is stopped, the whole goddamn state of Texas will belong to Owen Tate!"

A few of the men grimaced, their faces tightening in half sneers. A few others nodded glumly. It was clear they all shared the sheriff's sentiments about Owen Tate.

"I hear Tate's been having some trouble with the Spill brothers gang," Fargo said.

"Him and everybody else," Witchell added, shaking his head. "It's been five years since I came down here from St. Louis. And I've never seen it so bad."

"What do you mean?"

"Those rustlers have been terrorizing every herd passing this way," Buck said. "And if we don't catch 'em before the spring cattle drives, all the ranches south of here are going to find some new route to the Shawnee. We'd have a tough time in Deadwood, with no cowpokes passing through. Even if it is just once a year."

Fargo nodded. That explained why the sheriff was so hot on the trail of the Spill brothers. It wasn't to help out Owen Tate. That was for dead certain.

"That's sure a big reward out for them," Fargo added. The sheriff's eyes glittered for a brief instant, then went dark as if a candle had been extinguished. So, he was interested in the money, Fargo thought. But he was being careful to hide the fact.

"Yep," Witchell said, with no emotion in his voice. "And I'll get 'em too. You seen anything suspicious?"

"I guess the Spill brothers must be around. I saw a couple of hangings," Fargo said. Witchell's face remained perfectly impassive, but the eyes sharpened. "But maybe it was your posse catching up with some of those rustlers."

"Where were these hangings?" Buck asked, his voice cold.

Fargo hesitated, not liking the chill in Witchell's voice. Then he decided to answer. "One, probably from yesterday, over in that direction." Fargo pointed back toward the river. "No bodies. Just three ropes left on a branch."

"That's interesting," the sheriff said. Buck Witchell's voice was perfectly controlled and even, as smooth as his dark tanned face. But Fargo heard the cold calculation behind the few words.

"And I spotted another a few hours back, on the far side of Deadwood," Fargo added. "The four of them had . . . just died. They looked like cowpunchers to me. That must have been the Spill brother's work."

"That's right," Buck Witchell said smoothly. "That Spill gang has been lynching a whole lot of Tate's ranch hands. Too bad, isn't it? What else did you find out?" Buck asked. Once again, he was using his loud, commanding tone of voice.

"There wasn't anything else to find out." Fargo shrugged. He decided to leave out the part about the dying boy's words. That could get the sheriff even more interested than he was already. If he only knew more about the boy. Besides, he had promised to deliver the message only to Il Patrone, Owen Tate. But from what Witchell had said, it didn't sound too likely he would ever get to talk to the rich, land-grabbing rancher.

Fargo glanced up at the sheriff, who was studying his face closely. He suddenly feared his thoughts had been read by the sharp-eyed sheriff. But Fargo knew that during long years on the trail among strangers, he had trained his face to remain unresponsive to his own thoughts.

"I get the distinct impression you're hiding something," Buck Witchell said.

Fargo smiled. "Like I said, I'm just passing through. And Lucia tagged along to look for her sister."

"Then since you're going nowhere in a hurry, you won't mind coming back to Deadwood with us," Buck Witchell said. "I think you know something about these hangings that you're not telling me. And if not, well then, maybe the famous Trailsman could help us track down some of these rustlers."

Buck Witchell's voice was hard and cold as hail, and just as impossible to ignore. But if he went to Deadwood, Fargo was certain Witchell would carry out frontier justice, or rather, swift injustice. Witchell would never believe he had been going after the judge.

"Why, I'd be happy to help," Fargo answered. "But unfortunately I've got pressing business up in Dallas."

"I'd hate to have to insist," Buck Witchell said, his hand moving toward his pistol. There was a long moment of silence as Fargo calculated his chances.

"You win," Fargo said with a smile. "We'll come along." He'd find a way for them to escape. Of course the sheriff would wonder why he was trying to get away if he had nothing to hide.

The posse's horses began to draw up around them as they turned their mounts to head back toward Deadwood. Fargo edged Lucia over to the side of the trail away from the river. The chaparral was high and thick, a tangle of thickets just taller than a horse's head. They might be able to break away. They had to.

It would be hard on the horses, he thought. He had no doubt his pinto would be up to it. The black-and-white Ovaro had proved itself time and again in the worst situations. The question was, would Lucia's horse keep up? Fargo glanced at the chestnut. It was sturdy, bred to tough trail work under the worst conditions. But whether it would plunge into the dense brush was another question. Most horses would balk. He'd have to take that chance. It was their only possibility for escape.

They had just begun to ride, trotting easily along, toward the back of the posse, when Fargo saw their chance. With one swift movement, he leaned over, seized the reins of Lucia's mount, and spurred the Ovaro, plunging off the trail and into the tangle of sage. Instantly he dropped the reins of Lucia's horse.

"Keep your head down! Stay close behind me!" he shouted over his shoulder to Lucia as they dove into the thick branches. Behind him the men shouted angrily. Shots were fired, but over their heads. Warning shots. In an instant they were deep in the dense thicket, the Ovaro plunging fearlessly between the bushes, the branches and brambles scraping the sides of the horse and Fargo's arms. He looked back. The chestnut followed just fine, keeping close behind. Fargo kept his head low on his horse's neck as the rough branches scratched him. He was glad for the buckskin jacket and heavy jeans he wore. The bullets zinged about them through the brush. They were aiming low, shooting blind into the chaparral.

Over the pounding of hooves Fargo heard Lucia cry out in pain. She was wearing a buckskin jacket too, but her skirts might not be giving her legs much protection from the branches. There was a trick to drawing your body in toward your horse when riding through the brush.

"Keep your head down!" he shouted back at her. The Ovaro expertly dodged the large sage, finding footing. The shrubs scratched at Fargo's face. He heard more shooting behind him and then shouting. The sheriff's men were following, but by the sound of it, they were having difficulty making their horses follow.

The ground here was flat. Fargo and Lucia had enough of a lead that the posse couldn't see them if they kept their heads down.

It was time to detour, he decided. He jerked up short and pulled the nose of the Ovaro hard right. The horse wheeled and took off at a right angle. The chestnut whinnied and shied, but then followed on the new course.

If the sheriff's men hadn't spread out, he and Lucia would get past their advancing line and escape. Fargo wiped his cheek with one hand and felt the wetness of the blood from the scratches of the brambles.

After a few more minutes of hard riding and dodging bushes, Fargo heard the noise of pursuit coming over his left shoulder. The men had swept by, and he and Lucia had, for the moment, escaped. The cover was thinning, he saw to his dismay. Easier for the horses, but less protection for them. They rode on, the horses' sweat foaming in the hot sun.

Fargo squinted at the sun and then swung the Ovaro farther to the right until they galloped in a line due south, heading back toward the trail and the river, but several miles east from where they had plunged off the trail. Just as he was calculating that they should cross the Buckhorn Trail soon, the dusty track opened before them.

As the Ovaro galloped across it, followed by the chestnut, Fargo's eyes swept the trail. No one in sight. But they wouldn't be safe taking the open road. They'd have to stay in the brush until they were far away. They plunged again into the chaparral on the other side of the trail.

The going was easier, a gentle slope down to the river. But Fargo didn't like the hillside. By descending into the bowl of the Nueces River valley, they could be seen by any of the riders scanning the terrain from the higher land. Between the clumps of sage he sighted the dark ruffle of live oaks down by the water and headed for it. They would be less visible there, he decided, and could follow the river for a few miles.

But when they crashed out of the chaparral onto the flat sand beside the water, Fargo saw that they couldn't be more exposed. The stand of oak was on the far side of the river, which was Circle T land. Farther downstream the trees abruptly ended, and the land stretched bare along the riverbanks as far down as he could see.

On the other side of the Nueces he observed a low bank and then the long sloping plains of the Circle T Ranch. They'd have to cross, he realized. He didn't want to venture onto the ranch again, but if they followed the river farther, there would be no cover. If the posse split up into search parties, some would be sure to double back and search along the trail and the river.

"Oh, hell," Fargo said aloud.

Lucia drew up next to him, and he glanced across at her. Her face was covered with welts and streaked with blood. As he had feared, the branches had pulled her skirts up, and her bare knees and shins were bloodied and scratched from the branches.

"Sorry I couldn't think of an easier escape route," he said. "Does it hurt much?"

"It is nothing." Lucia winced. "It was worth it just to get away from them. Ha! I can't stand Buck Witchell. He's a bully. This will show him!"

Fargo smiled. "We're going to have to try to cross onto the ranch again. It's the only way."

"I know," she said.

Fargo scanned the river, spotted a bed of gravel, and spurred the Ovaro, which entered and crossed easily. Midstream he scooped up a hatful of water and poured it over his head, feeling the cold water sting the scratches on his face. Lucia followed.

Their horses emerged dripping on the opposite bank, and Fargo moved quickly into the cover of the stand of oak by the stream. He dismounted and let the pinto drink. Lucia did the same with the chestnut.

Fargo turned to survey the land across the river behind him. The nubby sage, flecked with tawny bald patches of dust, stood still in the blazing sun. No sign of the posse. They'd have to ride fast to be up over the bank and out of sight.

Lucia knelt beside the water, splashing it over her face. She unfastened her dark hair swiftly, combed it out, and fastened it up again with a few graceful movements. She hiked up her skirts and washed the blood from her scratched knees and shins, then unbuttoned her blouse and splashed the cool water on her neck and chest. As she stood up, Fargo saw the curve of one full breast through her still open blouse. She turned toward him, still buttoning her blouse. She noticed the direction of his eyes and smiled.

"This is a lot more dangerous than I thought it would be," he said. "I'm sorry that I let you come."

"I'm not," she said. "It's better than rotting in Deadwood. I hated that bar. And I wasn't making enough money to ever leave. They made sure of that. So you've done me a favor."

He smiled down at her. She came nearer. He touched one of the swollen welts across her cheek. The scratches were not too serious and would take only a few days to heal. "Hurt?" he asked.

She shook her head and smiled, her eyes dark and inviting. Fargo leaned over touched her lips with his, drinking in the sweet taste of her. He slipped his arms around her back as she pulled nearer to him, her round, soft breasts against his chest, the plumpness of her in his arms. After a moment he pulled free.

"Later?" he asked.

She nodded and smiled.

"We'll ride up this bank and across Circle T land for about five miles. With luck we won't run into any of the line riders from the ranch. Then we'll cross back over the river. That should put Witchell and his men off our trail for good."

She nodded and they mounted. Fargo took one last look back as he led them up the bank and onto the spreading land of the Circle T Ranch.

In half a mile the river fell away behind, and they rode across a flat plain of luxuriant grass, dotted only occasionally with gray green sage and mesquite. As they galloped, Fargo sighted tiny figures standing erect on the grass. He pointed them out to Lucia and swerved the Ovaro wide as the prairie dogs gave shrill calls and disappeared into their burrows. Nothing could snap a horse's leg faster than a misstep into a prairie dog hole, he thought. And even the best horse could accidentally step into one.

They galloped on, making good speed, Fargo's eyes alert for the line riders. He noted the scars of deep hoofprints and the close cropped grass where the cattle had grazed. The Circle T Ranch encompassed all of this, he thought, looking at the far horizon. And this was just one small corner.

The land began to roll in wide folds. The horses climbed the hills and plunged gracefully down them again, sweating in the heat. They would have to rest soon, Fargo realized. The horses had run hard. It was almost time to turn back toward the river. They had gone far enough east so that when they got back on the Buckhorn Trail, chances were they wouldn't meet any of the posse.

One more hill, he decided, and then they would turn north. The Ovaro galloped in long strides up the hillside followed by the chestnut, which was tiring. Just as they crested the rise, Fargo saw the pinto's ears flatten. The warning came too late.

Riding toward them up the hillside were a dozen men—cowpunchers, spread out in a long line. Three immediately drew their rifles as they sighted the two riders.

Fargo swore. It would do no good to try to outrun them. The pinto was tired, and the chestnut had been dragging for the last few miles. "We're going to have to talk our way out of it," he said in a low voice to Lucia.

"You're trespassing on Tate land," one of the cowboys shouted as they drew near. Some punchers immediately surrounded the two of them, and others galloped to the top of the hill, no doubt to see if other interlopers followed. They were careful. Professional, Fargo thought.

"How do, ma'am?" several of them said to Lucia, admiringly.

"This is Tate land? Really?" Fargo said innocently. "Is this the Circle T Ranch that I've heard so much about?"

"Sure is," one of the punchers said, a Mexican-looking boy. He eyed Lucia as he spoke. "Why we've got more land and longhorns than any other ranch in the country!" Fargo heard the unmistakable note of pride in his voice.

"But you're trespassing on Tate land!" another cut in. He was a brown-eyed kid with curly black hair.

"Well, I'm sorry I didn't realize where we were. We'd be happy to get off your land, if you can just point us in the right direction," Fargo said amiably. This was going well, he thought. Very well. They'd get an escort to the river. And that would be that.

"Sure," one of the cowboys said.

"Wait a minute!" another voice said excitedly. A skinny dark-skinned kid in an oversized hat spoke. "Isn't that Pablo's chestnut?"

Fargo swore silently to himself. He had forgotten for the moment that Lucia's horse was the one he had found near the first hanging. This was going to take some fancy explaining.

A thunderstorm of voices erupted, some in Spanish, others in English, as the punchers shouted and jockeyed for a view of Lucia's mount.

"He's right. It's branded Circle T!" another shouted. A chorus of angry voices echoed.

"Hanging's what we do in Texas when a man steals a horse," the black-haired one said threateningly.

"I didn't steal it," Fargo said. "It was wandering. I was about to give it back to you once I realized this was the Circle T." He hoped the lie sounded convincing.

The punchers eyed him, some of them nodding. The black-haired kid still looked suspicious. "I think we'd better herd you back to the line camp," the kid said. "You'll have to talk to Hank."

Fargo nodded. There was no choice. The cowpunchers drew up around him and Lucia, and they set off. There was no possibility for escape, Fargo realized. No brush to ride into. And the Ovaro was tired. Even so, it could probably outrun the puncher's horses. But Lucia's chestnut couldn't. And he couldn't leave Lucia behind. Who knew what might happen to her on the Tate ranch? And she was his one reliable witness to what had happened in Deadwood.

They had traveled only a mile over the open prairie, heading toward the interior of the ranch, when they came to the line camp. It consisted of a board shack, a fire pit, a water pump and trough, and a corral. This was the headquarters for the line riders. Fargo knew that the big ranches had such outposts every fifteen miles or so around the perimeter of the ranch. The punchers rode the border as a kind of living fence over the vast distances to keep the cattle in . . . and, in the case of the Tate ranch, visitors out.

As they rode up, Fargo saw a pot-bellied man leaning against the corral. His skinny legs were long and awkward. He wore a battered tan hat and plaid shirt. When he walked toward them, he reminded Fargo of an oversized, top-heavy chicken. Skye smiled, in spite of himself.

"What are you grinning at, stranger?" the pot-bellied man growled.

Fargo and Lucia dismounted, along with three of the cowpunchers. The others remained mounted.

"I thought I recognized you," Fargo said. That wasn't a lie. "But I see I was mistaken. My name's Skye Fargo. You must be Hank." Fargo held out his hand, but the pot-bellied man merely looked at it.

"What are you doing on the Circle T?"

"He's stole Pablo's horse for one thing!" one of the cowpunchers cut in. Hank started and glanced over at the chestnut.

"Well, that could explain a lot," Hank rasped. "I got some bad news for you, boys."

"Not Pablo!" one of them said.

"And Ross, and Luke, and Sandy," Hank said, his voice hard.

There was a long silence. Fargo heard a mockingbird far off.

"Goddamn," one of the punchers said, stamping the ground.

They must have been the four cowboys Fargo had found hanged. And the one who had given him the message, the one who looked Mexican, was probably Pablo, the same one who owned the chestnut.

"So you must know something about all this," Hank said. "That's how you got Pablo's horse."

"I found it wandering," Fargo said, "west of Deadwood. I would have returned it to you."

Hank grunted and took a few steps forward until he stood next to the chestnut. He put his hand upon the empty saddle. He glanced across at Fargo's pinto, started, and then a slow smile spread across his face. "And what's this?" he asked, advancing on the horse. He pulled the woven leather reata from Fargo's saddle.

"I found that in a bush," Fargo explained. "By the river maybe ten miles back."

Hank's eyes narrowed as he held up the lariat. "This belonged to Carlos," he said. One of the punchers nodded assent, and the rest muttered.

"Tie him up, boys," Hank said. "Mr. Owen Tate will be real happy when I bring him the man who's been responsible for the murder of his ranch hands."

4

"Murder?" Fargo said. "That's ridiculous!"

Two of the cowpunchers stepped forward immediately and seized Fargo's arms. He tensed, ready to resist, ready to draw his pistol, and then thought better of it. They had him outnumbered and outgunned. He didn't want to kill anybody; he'd just go willingly. For the moment.

The punchers held him tightly, one of them lifting his Colt out of its holster. Fargo thought of the throwing knife strapped to his ankle. He hoped they'd miss that.

"I've got a real strong suspicion you're the one responsible for all those hangings," Hank spat. "And I'll bet Mr. Tate is going to be real glad when I bring you to him."

"Come to think of it, I'd like to talk to Mr. Owen Tate," Fargo said evenly. He had a sudden inspiration. "In fact I might even have some information for him." By the time he got to see Tate, he thought, he might know what the dying boy's message meant. Then he could decide whether to deliver the real thing, or make up something else.

Hank's eyes narrowed and he took a step closer to Fargo. "What kind of information?"

"That's for me to tell Mr. Tate. Or Il Patrone, that is, in person."

Hank glared at him. "I don't believe you have information. I think you'd tell any kind of lie just to save your own neck. Well, it's not going to work."

Hank suddenly drew back his fist and slugged Fargo in the belly. Skye saw it coming and tightened the muscles of his stomach, but even so, the breath left him and his head reeled. Lucia cried out. The cowpokes on either side of him held him up as he stumbled backward from the blow.

"You like that, do you?" Hank asked. Fargo shook his head to clear it.

"Not much," he muttered. "Look, I didn't have anything to do with these hangings you're talking about. Nothing. Understand?"

Hank drew back his fist, and the cowpokes tightened their grips on Fargo.

"No!" Lucia screamed, but the blow was an uppercut, and Fargo's head snapped back as the pain radiated hot along his jaw. He slumped forward and felt Hank step up to him. Another blow fell heavy on the back of his head and, after a fountain of shattered stars, all went black.

His head throbbed. He felt his arms painfully restrained above his head with his back up against rough boards. Even with his eyes closed, he realized he was being held inside the shack. He moved his head from one side to the other to loosen his neck muscles. Then he slowly opened his eyes.

He sat on the dirt floor of the supply shack. Dull light of sunset filtered through the walls and threw red stripes on the wooden kegs and shelves holding burlap bags. The shack was small but kept the camp's supplies out of the rain. Time had passed since he'd lost consciousness. He smelled fire smoke and coffee. The red light grew dimmer and finally faded away. The sun had set. He heard voices outside and the rattle of pans. Suppertime.

Fargo stretched his cramped muscles and then pulled his legs together in front of him, rubbing one ankle against the other. The knife was still there. He smiled to himself. It would be possible to escape after dark, he thought. The question was, could he manage to get Lucia away with him? He glanced up at his hands and cursed inwardly.

Each wrist was secured by a ring of a set of handcuffs, the other ring locked around a horizontal pole that formed part of the shack's structure. His eyes explored the handcuffs and the pole, but there was no way to get loose. His knife wouldn't help him out after all.

What kind of cowboy would be carrying two sets of handcuffs on the range? The question reminded him of the sheriff's comments about Owen Tate and his slaves. Was that the Circle T secret? Did Tate keep everybody off the ranch because he was using slaves to drive the cattle? Even though slavery was legal in the state of Texas, most ranchers used hired hands for the cattle drives. A rancher couldn't keep an eye on cattle and slaves at the same time. And it just wasn't the way ranching was done.

The tradition of cowpunchers followed that of the free vaqueros of Mexico. It was a good system, Fargo thought. The punchers hired on for the spring cattle drives, which kept them employed until autumn. Then some of them stayed on the ranch for the winter, and the rest found odd jobs in the towns. In the spring it was time for the roundup, the branding of the calves, and driving the herds north to market.

An expert cowpuncher made enough of a living that he could own a ranch in time. Of course a lot of cowboys had no interest in settling down. They were content to make the spring drives year after year, spend their money in the saloons and gaming houses, and live the free life of roaming.

Still, Fargo thought, noting the handcuffs again in the gathering darkness, he would keep his eyes open. He listened to the sounds outside the shack, and he strained to hear Lucia's voice. He hoped they were treating her right.

It was dark enough outside now that he could see the golden light of the fire filtering between the cracks in the boards. The smell of beans and bacon wafted to his nostrils, and he heard his stomach growl. It had been a long time since he'd had a meal.

He heard footsteps of two people approaching, and the door creaked open. Lucia stood on the threshold with the black-haired cowpoke, who held a plate of steaming chow and a mug of coffee.

"Skye!" she exclaimed. She hurried to his side and dabbed at his face with a handkerchief. "How are you feeling?"

"I'll be better if I can get my hands free and have some dinner," he answered. "How about unlocking these things?"

The cowboy shook his head warily. "Strict instructions," he said. "Hank said leave you fastened. He rode off to check on the north perimeter. And he's the only one who's got the keys."

"Great," Fargo shot at him. "Suppose this shack caught fire? Would you just let me roast in here?"

The cowpoke shook his head again. "Never did think of that," he admitted. "Then you'd be in a fine fix. But you deserve it if you're the one responsible for those hangings—"

"I told you, I had nothing to do with it!"

"Yeah," the kid said. "I almost believe you when you say that. But we've been having a hard time out here. The rest of the boys are . . . well, scared. And Hank, he's convinced you're responsible. He's real convinced of that."

"On what grounds?" Fargo asked. "Because I found a horse wandering? Because I found somebody's lariat in a bush? If I was guilty, do you think I'd come riding onto the Circle T? And how do you think one man can hang four of your punchers?"

"You've some good points," the puncher said, stroking his beardless chin. "Well, Mr. Tate will know what to do with you. That's for certain."

"Meanwhile, how am I supposed to eat with my arms hanging up here?" Fargo asked. If there was some way to needle the kid to get the cuffs loose from the support beam . . .

"Guess Miss Lucia will have to feed you," the puncher said. "I can tell you a dozen men who wouldn't mind being in that position . . ." The puncher blushed, placed the food on a barrel, and backed out of the door, closing it behind him.

"They're all just boys," Lucia said, as she fetched the food and brought it near. "And good boys too. Except for Hank, of course." She lifted a forkful of beans to Fargo's mouth. It was good. Some of the best cooking in the West took place on the open range, Fargo thought as he ate.

"I don't like Hank one bit," she spat. "He's already decided you're guilty."

Fargo nodded and grunted between bites.

"One of the boys told me that for a couple of months, groups of the line riders have been murdered . . . hanged."

"The ropes we saw on the tree," Fargo said, nodding. "And I saw some punchers hanged before I got to Deadwood. Near where I picked up the chestnut."

Lucia shivered as she lifted another forkful of the stew toward him.

"Another thing I found out," she continued, "they all think the Spill gang is responsible. In fact, Hank's been sending out the line riders all over to try to intercept them. Curly—he's the one who just brought in the food—has a real respect for that gang. He says no matter which way they ride, the Spill gang is always in the opposite direction."

Fargo nodded, deep in thought.

Lucia spoke again. "So now Hank has a new suspect to add to the Spill brothers."

"Me. Well, I guess Mr. Tate will decide what to do," Fargo said, echoing Curly's words. "I'm looking forward to meeting the famous Il Patrone. Tomorrow could get interesting." He thought for a moment. "Look," he added, "you don't have to stick around. You might be able to slip away tonight. Ride out. Find your sister."

"Or the judge in Brownwater," she said thoughtfully. "But if the sheriff found out you were here before I got back, there'd be nobody to say what really happened with the deputy. They'd hang you for sure."

"That's true," Fargo said. "I just don't want you dragged into this more than you are already."

She thought for a moment. "I think I'll stick around. Besides," she added, "I'm as curious as you are about Owen Tate. And that's another strange thing." Lucia lifted the cooling coffee to his lips. "In Deadwood all I heard about Mr. Tate is what a mean man he is. But these cowboys think the world of him. Why, this afternoon they were showing me the remuda and bragging about how

Mr. Tate always buys the best horses for them. They were telling me about the longhorns they're about to drive north. Why, to hear their pride, you'd think they owned the ranch themselves!"

"Interesting," Fargo said. It didn't match the picture of Owen Tate that the sheriff had portrayed, a slave-driving, avaricious bastard. Well, he'd know soon enough when he met the man.

Meanwhile he had something else to worry about. If word came from Deadwood that Skye Fargo was wanted for the shooting of the deputy, the ranch hands would turn him over to Buck Witchell. His only hope was to settle this with Owen Tate as soon as possible and get on his way before the message arrived.

The coffee was finished and Lucia stood. "I'll be back," she said with a smile. She left and Fargo heard her voice outside talking to the cowboys. Then she reentered carrying Fargo's bedroll and a couple of blankets.

"Let me see if I can make you more comfortable."

"A key to these handcuffs would help a lot," Fargo muttered. His arms, held above his head, were beginning to throb. It was damned uncomfortable. He felt anger welling up in him, and he imagined his arms free and the awkward chicken figure of Hank standing in front of him. He pushed the anger down. Later. He'd get him later.

Lucia arranged the bedroll under him and behind his back. Then she spread blankets out on the dirt floor beside him for her own bed.

"That is better," he said. It was dark in the shack, but the golden light from the campfire filtered in between the warped boards. She sat down on the blanket and unbound her hair, combing it out. She was damned pretty, he thought as he watched her.

"How about a good-night kiss?" he asked.

Lucia glanced over at him and smiled. "We could do better than that," she said, leaning up against him and snuggling under his chin.

"I'm afraid not tonight," he said, nodding his head toward his handcuffed wrists. She leaned over and kissed him, her warm lips soft and sweet. He slipped his tongue gently, exploringly into her mouth, and she moaned low. He felt himself harden with anticipation, ready for her. Inwardly he cursed the blasted handcuffs. He continued to probe her mouth with his tongue, and she leaned closer to him, rubbing her round soft breasts against his chest.

"Whoa," he said softly. "I didn't know you were going to come in here and torture me."

"Aren't you enjoying it?" she asked, a smile in her voice. She pulled away and slowly began to unbutton her blouse, and he saw her large swelling breasts emerge, with large dark areolas and nipples.

"Dessert?" he muttered as she raised herself above him, and he nuzzled his head between the silken soft curves, turning his head to take one nipple into his mouth and then the other. She moaned again, then stifled it. Her smooth flesh smelled of herbs, and the nipples hardened in his mouth as he flicked his tongue over them rapidly.

Fargo felt Lucia's hand trail down across his broad muscular chest, stopping to unbutton his shirt and slipping inside to caress him. He felt himself straining against his jeans. God*damn* the handcuffs.

Her hips had begun a gentle undulation, and she began to rub her hard pubis rhythmically against his thigh. He moved his leg gently, forcing it between her legs with each of her pumping motions. Her breasts swayed against his face as he caught one then another nipple in his mouth.

"Oh, Skye," she murmured. Her hand dropped down to his belly, and she slowly undid his Levi's. She gasped as he pushed up, erect, huge, and hard, ready for her.

"Oh!" she exclaimed. She stroked his shaft with one hand as she unfastened her skirt and pulled off her bloomers with the other. She was stark naked now, her full round breasts above her tiny waist and rounded hips. He strained against the cuffs again, eager to touch her. The dark triangle of fur parted as she knelt above his erectness. Then, with exquisite slowness, she lowered herself onto him, inch by inch, burying his shaft into her wet tightness.

At last he could stand no more, and he thrust upward, plunging into her as she gasped. He bucked up and down like a bronco as she rode him, her breasts bouncing, her face raised toward the rafters in ecstasy.

"Oh!" Lucia whispered, trying to keep her voice low. "Oh God. You're so big. Oh God, more, more."

He pumped harder into her, grinding against her wet pubis until she jammed her fist into her mouth in an effort to keep quiet. Then he saw her strain against him and knew she was close, her gasps coming closer and closer as he felt the gathering inside himself. Suddenly her back arched, and she gasped. He felt her contractions on him, strong, and he felt the explosion rising, coming, shooting into her as he arched up, pumped once, twice, three times, four, giving all of himself into her.

Lucia fell forward onto his chest and lay still,

panting. Fargo longed to put his arms around her. After a few minutes her breathing slowed, and she stirred and looked up at him.

"I'm looking forward to next time, when I have my hands free," he said, straining his head forward to kiss her hair.

"If . . . if there is a next time," she whispered. "I'm worried about you. Hank is . . . is talking about avenging the deaths of those cowboys. I don't understand what he's got against you that he's so convinced you're guilty."

"Sometimes fear can do that to a man," Fargo said as she nuzzled up under his chin. "They're all afraid because of what's been happening. And looking for somebody to blame. Anybody." And wouldn't it be just his luck to be that somebody, he thought. "Don't worry," he murmured. "Everything will turn out all right."

But as he lay listening to Lucia's breathing deepen into sleep, he felt the throbbing pain begin again in his arms. He realized he had said that as much to assure himself as her.

The clatter of pans woke him, and he saw the pale yellow dawn leaking into the supply shack. He shifted his long, lean body. Lucia, half covered by a blanket and lying across him, stirred in her sleep. Fargo felt fresh pain along his shoulders and arms. What a stupid inhumane way to hold a prisoner, he thought. He spent a few minutes clenching and unclenching his fists to get the blood pumping through them. It was hard going, the tingling sensation running along his arms and into his tight neck. After a while though his muscles felt better.

He heard footsteps approaching the shack, and then the door opened. Curly stood there, squinting into the darkness of the shed. He opened his mouth to stay something and then saw Lucia's nakedness as she lay on Fargo. Curly closed his mouth again and his eyes widened. Fargo gave him a wink and said "Sh." Curly blinked several times and closed the door again.

Lucia turned and raised her head. "What was that?" she said sleepily.

"That was your friend Curly putting his head in the door. I think your reputation is ruined forever."

"And yours is made," she said with a giggle. "Well, let's see what's cooking." She rose.

"See if you can talk Hank into getting me out of these shackles," Fargo said.

She dressed quickly, bound up her hair, and left. Fargo heard her outside and Hank's voice answering. The campfire crackled. The smell of coffee and smoke tingled his nose. Then he heard footsteps again, and Hank opened the door. He entered, followed by Curly. Hank held a pistol in front of him, aimed at Fargo.

"Don't try anything cute," Hank said, handing the clinking keys to Curly. "Just loosen the rings around the post. Leave the cuffs on him." The cowpoke approached warily and fumbled with the locks on the handcuffs. One arm was freed and then the other. Fargo lowered them slowly, feeling the rush of blood and pain. The muscles across his shoulders were tense, and he stretched slowly.

"Get up," Hank said.

Fargo rose to his feet, and Hank gestured for him to go outside, following and covering him with the pistol. Lucia was washing up at the water pump. Six of the cowpokes sat around the fire while the cook poured coffee and flipped oatcakes. The punchers looked up as Fargo emerged, and he could tell from their expressions—ranging from un-abashed envy to embarrassed smirks—that Curly had told them what he had seen.

"Nice bunkhouse," Fargo said to them. "One of the best night's sleep I've had in a long time." One of the punchers guffawed, and another dug him in the ribs with his elbow.

Hank let him wash up and then motioned him toward a wagon not far from the fire circle. Fargo sat as commanded, and Hank snapped one of the rings around a spoke on the wheel of the wagon. Lucia brought him coffee and oatcakes, and he ate one-handed, enjoying the freedom of his arms.

After breakfast Hank gave the orders for the day. Four of the punchers were to relieve the night riders while two would accompany Hank to bring Fargo and Lucia to Owen Tate at the hacienda. Fargo noted that when Hank spoke of going to see Tate, he puffed his chest out even more, making his spindly legs look all the more ridiculous. The punchers all seemed to want to be chosen to go the hacienda, but Hank was firm in his selection. One was Curly and the other was named Juan.

The four line riders selected their horses for the day and saddled them while Lucia watched. After further instructions from Hank they rode out.

While the cook cleaned up from breakfast, Hank filled a pot of water and hung a small mirror from a nail on the shack and, stripped to the waist, his belly overhanging his belt, he proceeded to shave.

Despite one shackled wrist, Fargo found he could do push-ups by angling his body close to the wagon. The exercise relieved the pain in his arms and shoulders. After a while he stopped and rested, watching Hank shave. The mirror flashed in the morning sun, throwing a sharp light against Hank's lathered face. Hank squinted into the glare, then moved so that he wasn't in the sun's reflection.

"What's with the handcuffs?" Fargo asked. "Pretty strange equipment for a ranch hand."

Hank's razor paused for a moment, and one eye looked balefully into the mirror at Fargo.

"Got 'em from an old friend of mine," Hank growled. "They come in real handy sometimes when we catch somebody the likes of you."

"That happen often?" Fargo asked. Hank grunted and didn't answer. After a few minutes Fargo tried again. "What's your take on the Spill brothers? I heard they're giving you a lot of trouble cattle rustling." He decided not to mention Buck Witchell, afraid that Hank might get curious about how he'd run into the sheriff. But Hank acted as though he hadn't heard anything. He continued to shave.

Finally Hank finished, rinsed the razor, and then took the mirror down and put it into his saddlebag. Curly and Juan were in the final stages of saddling and packing the horses. Juan put the saddle blanket on the Ovaro, and Fargo saw that several folds of the blanket were not smoothed out. If uncorrected, after a few hours the pinto would have saddle sores.

"Careful," Fargo said. "Get that blanket straight."

Juan turned his head and grinned.

"Hold on, Señor Fargo," he said. "I haven't finished here. I never galled a horse since I was riding. And I was riding before I was walking!" Fargo nodded his head as he saw Juan smooth the blanket down, then lift the saddle onto the pinto and cinch it snugly. It was well done, he had to admit.

"Just watching out for my horse," Fargo said.

"No offense taken," Juan answered. "A good man worries about what's under his saddle. That's what Il Patrone says all the time. And we follow his example." The tone of reverence in Juan's voice was unmistakable. Fargo wondered what Owen Tate would really be like.

When the horses were ready, Hank approached Fargo and drew his pistol again. At Hank's instruction Curly unlocked the handcuff from the wagon wheel, then snapped it onto Fargo's other wrist in front of him. Lucia had mounted and stood waiting. The punchers held the pinto for him and helped him as Fargo awkwardly mounted, slithering up the saddle, using his shackled hands.

"I'm going to be riding right behind you," Hank said. "So don't try anything. Either of you."

Fargo looked across at Lucia and nodded. Escape didn't look likely, he thought.

They rode across the open range, the wide loping hills giving way gradually to flat grassland. Fargo's keen eyes caught sight of a cloud of dust smudging the horizon.

The Ovaro's ears pricked, and Fargo's keen hearing caught the distant roll of cattle lowing. After a few more miles they rode alongside the herd, which was strung out along a creek as far as the eye could see.

Fargo observed the herd. Most of the cattle were longhorns, the dusky, tall native cattle that ran wild on the plains and never seemed to need water. But mixed among the longhorns were low-slung red Herefords. Some of the new calves showed traits of both breeds.

Fargo sighted some punchers riding in the distance on the other side of the herd. They spotted Hank's group and waved, then galloped away in the opposite direction. As on most ranches, Fargo knew, the herd was free to roam the interior, the cowboys merely watching over them and rescuing the occasional calf stuck in a ravine. But sometime soon, in midspring, the ranch hands would round up the cattle, brand the new calves, cut the herd, and drive some north along the Shawnee Trail.

Fargo measured the herd as they rode along. He had no doubt this was but one of many herds on the ranch. He noted the numerous new calves among the beeves and cows. A herd could double every three years. And one head might bring as much as $25, delivered. Ranching was one hell of a lucrative business, he thought. Owen Tate was a fabulously wealthy man. He wondered what Tate was like—the avaricious land-grabber Buck Witchell had told him about, or the kindly patron Juan looked up to? Well, he'd find out soon enough. And his life might depend on the answer.

They passed the herd finally and continued along the creek for another hour, coming at last to a low adobe settlement situated under huge live oaks. Whitewashed dwellings lined either side of a broad main street, partly shaded by the trees. The warm smell of cooking tortillas wafted on the shade-cooled air.

The five of them rode down the street. Women in colorful skirts and shawls tended large plots of cultivated vegetables. Some of the women waved as they passed. It sure didn't look like slavery, Fargo thought.

"Is . . . is this the hacienda?" Lucia asked, looking about her.

Juan, riding nearby, chuckled. "Oh, no, señorita," he assured her. "We live here. Well the ones who are part of the ranch. The hacienda is a few miles away."

Lucia continued to look about her. Suddenly Fargo saw her stiffen as if she had been shot.

"Lucia?" he called out. Abruptly, before anyone could stop her, she leaped down from her horse and ran toward a group of women in a garden nearby. She was shouting inarticulately.

Fargo watched helplessly, his hands cuffed, as Hank called after Lucia to stop and then drew his pistol. But Lucia was already hugging one of the women, and they were both speaking excitedly in Spanish. The other women watched them in amazed silence. Hank slowly holstered his gun. Fargo knew Lucia had found her sister. From the rapid fire of their speaking, Fargo gathered Lucia was asking Angelina all about the ranch. After a few moments Lucia turned back toward the mounted men.

"Skye! It's Angelina! She is here," Lucia shouted, her voice still quavering with excitement.

The women began to walk toward them, Lucia and Angelina in the lead, their arms still around each other as if reluctant to let go. Angelina, a slender version of Lucia, spoke rapidly to them in Spanish, which Fargo could follow. She was asking that Lucia be allowed to remain with her.

"I can't leave that girl with you," Hank answered. "I caught her trespassing on the ranch. She's coming along with this character"—he nodded his head toward Fargo—"to see Mr. Tate."

A babble of women's voices rose in protest, and Hank covered his ears.

"That should not be necessary, if it is Angelina's sister," Juan cut in.

"Oh, all right," Hank said after a moment. "I'll leave her with you. But mind she doesn't get into any trouble."

Lucia approached Fargo as he sat on the pinto. The tears of joy were still in her eyes. "I will stay here with Angelina. When you need me . . . for . . ." She paused, looking up at him and not wanting to mention the shooting of the deputy in front of the others. "Send a message and I will come. I will be safe here with my sister. She says she is very happy here on the ranch. There are many people from our town of Piedritas. Thank you for bringing me along. Without you I never would have found my Angelina." Lucia gave her sister a squeeze.

"Just luck," Fargo said. And with a little more luck he'd get clear of this ranch quickly and get to Brownwater and to the circuit judge. He could travel more quickly without Lucia along anyway. Then he'd send a message to her to come for the trial. "You'll be hearing from me," he said.

Lucia nodded. "And I will come immediately," she said.

The four of them rode on under the oaks, the chestnut tethered behind them. The stream gurgled and curved between cut banks of yellow earth. Soon Fargo saw low buildings surrounded by an adobe wall on the top of a gentle rise.

They rode through a wide wooden gate and entered a huge yard. On one side he saw stables and a corral in which sleek ponies galloped around and around. Other buildings, storehouses from the looks of them, crowded along the periphery. In the center rose the main house, a broad and tall adobe structure, the brown mud walls pierced by lines of wooden rafters that supported the red tile roof. All around the house ran a deep covered ramada with rough-hewn chairs and tables and clay pots of green plants.

A short, rotund man hurried out of the house,

followed by two others. Hank dismounted, along with Curly and Juan. Fargo slid down off the Ovaro, and their horses were led away.

"Who is this?" the short man asked, nodding toward Fargo. He had a heavy Spanish accent.

"None of your business," Hank snapped. "I need to see Mr. Tate. Immediately."

The short man drew himself up to his full height. "Not until I know who this is you are bringing to see him."

Hank spat at the man's feet, just missing his boot. "Look, Diego," Hank said impatiently. "Just tell Mr. Tate that I need to see him. It's important."

"Mr. Tate is very busy at the moment," Diego replied, unimpressed. "So first you must tell me what your business is."

"Hell," Hank said. "Used to be I could see Mr. Tate whenever I wanted to. Now he's so important . . ." he muttered under his breath.

"Who are you?" Diego shot at Fargo. "What are you doing here?"

"My name's Skye Fargo," he answered.

"You tell Mr. Tate," Hank cut in, "that we lost four more men—Pablo, Ross, Luke, and Sandy."

Fargo noted how cold Hank's voice had become. Diego winced at the names and bit his lip.

"And I caught this fellow with Pablo's horse. And he had that lariat that belonged to Carlos too. So you go in there and tell Mr. Tate that I'm bringing him somebody who probably knows what happened to those men. Hell, I bet he's even responsible. And you tell Mr. Tate that if he just gives the word, I'll string this bastard up fast."

Diego looked at Fargo sharply. "I see what you mean," he said slowly to Hank. "I will have to ask

73

if Mr. Tate has time to see you." Diego turned quickly and reentered the house.

"Has time? Has time to see me?" Hank muttered, pacing back and forth. Curly and Juan shifted nervously.

"This is uncomfortable," Fargo said, moving his wrists inside the shackles. "Think you could uncuff me now?" He'd need his hands free if things got ugly. That was for damned sure.

Hank glanced at him and smiled thinly. "You're going to be a damned sight more uncomfortable when I get through with you," he said. But the words were hollow and cruel, not vengeful. Fargo suddenly realized that it wasn't anger about what had happened to his men that was motivating Hank. It was something else. Something more complicated, more dangerous.

"What have you got against me?" Fargo asked him. "You don't really believe I had anything to do with those hangings, do you?"

"Bullshit." Hank spat and turned away.

Curly shot him a sympathetic look. Before Fargo had a chance to press Hank again, Diego returned.

"Come with me," he said. Diego led, Fargo followed, and the others brought up the rear. As they crossed the ramada and came to the thick wooden door, Diego motioned to the two young boys. "You two stay here." Curly and Juan looked relieved and dejected both at once.

Fargo heard Hank draw his pistol as they entered the hacienda. Ridiculous, he thought. Hank was bringing a handcuffed man to Mr. Tate, but he still wanted to show off by waving his gun around.

They walked through a magnificently wide room with a huge stone fireplace. Bearskin rugs were scattered on the planked floor, and the walls were covered with colorful Indian blankets and antelope, buffalo and moose head trophies. Diego led them down a short hallway and then opened a door.

Fargo entered the study where books covered the walls and a wooden desk dominated one end of the room. The tall leather desk chair was turned away from them.

"Here we are," Diego said. The desk chair began to turn toward them slowly, squeaking in protest.

And then she stood gracefully, rising out of the chair, rising out of his memories, her lithe form as graceful as it had been all those years ago in St. Louis, her pale gold hair piled on her head and her eyes bright with expectation.

"Skye!" she exclaimed. "Skye Fargo! I couldn't believe it when Diego told me you had come. It's been years. What a surprise!" She glanced down at his manacled hands. "Take those off him!" she snapped at Hank.

Hank scurried forward and unfastened the cuffs, shooting dirty looks at Fargo. Hank stepped back.

"Faith," Fargo said. "Faith Lawrence. What are you doing here?"

"Faith Tate," she said with a smile. "Mrs. Owen Tate."

5

Faith Lawrence Tate crossed the wide room lightly like a half-forgotten dream, opening her arms to him, her warmth and softness reminding him that she was real as he folded her against his chest and brushed his lips against her fragrant hair, telling himself that now she was another man's wife. And not just any man's, Owen Tate's.

Hank cleared his throat loudly, and Faith stepped out of Fargo's arms.

"You . . . you know this character, Miz Tate?" Hank asked hesitantly.

Faith's laugh danced like a ripple on silver water. "Know him?" she repeated. "Why, Skye Fargo and I go way back."

"Well, he knows something about the hangings, Miz Tate," Hank said darkly. "In fact, I think he may be responsible."

Faith's face grew immediately sober, and a look of pain came into her wide eyes. "What do you mean by that, Hank?" Her voice was suddenly sharp like the leap of an antelope.

"I'd like to discuss this directly with Mr. Tate," said Hank, crossing his arms.

"You'll discuss it with me. Now," Faith said. "Mr. Tate can't see you just at the moment. Tell me what you know, and I'll relay it to him. I promise."

Hank shifted from one foot to another and then softened. "Well, I caught him trespassing on our land," he said.

"A lot of folks trespass on the Circle T," she said shortly.

"And he had that reata that belonged to Carlos. And Pablo's chestnut."

"Pablo's . . . wait a minute," Faith said, a catch in her voice. "Where is Pablo?"

"Him too, Miz Tate," Hank said, his voice cold. "Yesterday I found him and Ross, Luke, and Sandy. Strung up, all four of 'em on a tree, blowing in the wind. Way over on the other side of Deadwood."

Faith's hand flew to her throat as the color drained out of her face. She took a faltering step backward and sank down onto the leather chair. She buried her face in her hands.

"Not Pablo too," she said, her voice muffled by sobs. "And Sandy and Ross. And Luke. I can't stand any more of it. When will it all stop? All our boys. Dead. All our boys . . ."

Fargo looked down at her as she shook with silent sobs, wishing there was something he could say, wishing there were a way to take away the kind of pain that she obviously felt. And something nagged at him. Something about this bothered him, but he couldn't quite place it. Hank looked away, out the wide window behind the desk, his eyes dark and unreadable. After a moment he glanced back at Faith and caught Fargo looking at him.

"And this man knows something, ma'am," Hank said. "Or else how come he would have a horse from one hanging and a lariat from a hanging that happened nearly a week before?"

Faith wiped her face with her handkerchief and

looked up at Skye with red-rimmed eyes. But there were only questions, not suspicions.

"I told you," Fargo said calmly to Hank, his eyes on Faith. "I found the chestnut wandering not far from the hanging. And I found the lariat in a bush near the river."

"Not likely!" Hank cut in.

"Oh, Hank," Faith said, "Skye Fargo is as honest as the ranch is big. If he says that's what happened, it did."

"I still say he's guilty," Hank said. "And I want to tell my suspicions to Mr. Tate. To his face."

"That's enough," Faith said firmly. "You've done your job by bringing him here. I assure you, Mr. Tate and I will deal with Mr. Fargo. You are dismissed."

"But . . ." Hank's fury reddened his face and, with his protruding belly and gawky legs, he looked more like poultry than ever. Faith nodded her head at Hank. He retrieved the handcuffs from the table and began to back away toward the door. "Just keep an eye on him," Hank said. "Or you'll be sorry." He left abruptly, and Fargo heard the metallic clank of the cuffs grow fainter as he retreated down the hall and left the hacienda. Hank slammed the heavy door behind him. Faith smiled at the sound.

"What did you do to him?" she asked.

"He just took an immediate dislike to me," he said with a shrug.

"Skye Fargo . . ." she said musingly, her eyes sweeping his long, lean body. She smiled wistfully. "It's been so many years. What brings you to Texas?"

"Just passing through on the way to New Orleans for a little relaxation. I happened across the hanging. Then I stopped in Deadwood to try to find out what it was all about." He decided to leave out the part about shooting the deputy. He'd tell her about that later. "And I rode out with a young barmaid named Lucia, who was trying to find her sister."

Faith smiled. "If there's a woman within a hundred miles, you'll find her," she said.

Fargo was surprised to hear a note of jealousy in Faith's voice, barely audible, like the distant yearning call of a mourning dove. After all she was a married woman. But apparently that hadn't ended her feelings for him.

"Where is this girl now?"

"She found her sister, Angelina, at the settlement west of here."

"That must be Angelina Alvarez," Faith said with a smile. "Angelina told me she had written to her sister in Mexico, but the letter was never answered. She was very worried. Well, I'm glad they found each other. Something good has come of all this." She sighed deeply, and Fargo heard the weight of something terrible in it. It was the hangings, he knew. But something more. There was a sadness about her. She smiled after a moment, as if to dispel the mood.

"And you're here, Skye," Faith said. "And that's the best thing that's happened to me for a long long time. Five years ago, in St. Louis, I had some trouble with, well, a suitor."

"Well, Faith, you never lacked for male attention," he put in with a chuckle.

"I could have done without this particular attention," she said. "This was one of those persistent bastards who just wouldn't let me be. I came down to Texas to get away from him and ended up in Deadwood, out of money. And damn if he didn't show up again, still chasing me. And that's when I met Owen." Fargo saw a look of pain flash across her face. Then she forced a smile. "And he saved me. He . . . is a wonderful man, kind and generous. He gave me a job here at the hacienda and . . . well, a month later, we married."

Fargo nodded, wondering if the pain was dissatisfaction with her marriage, or something else. She sounded sincere when she described Tate as wonderful. He knew Faith well enough to read her, and she wasn't pretending. So what was going on?

"I'm looking forward to meeting Owen . . . your husband," he said. It was a lucky man who had won Faith Lawrence, he thought. She was beautiful as a clear dawn, smart, level-headed and all woman.

"He's . . . upstairs working at the moment," Faith said. "I'm sure he'll be down to see us later. Or tomorrow. Please stay with us for a while." He heard the distance yearning in her voice again.

"I've got to get a move on," Fargo said and then made a sudden decision. "But I do have a message for Mr. Tate. It's urgent. I promised a dying man I'd deliver it directly to Il Patrone and no one else." Fargo was more and more curious to meet the man who owned this ranch and had won Faith Lawrence.

"A message?" she asked. "Can you tell me?"

Fargo hesitated.

"I promised to tell only Il Patrone and no one else. The man said that other people's lives depended on that."

Faith's face lost its color. "I see. Let me go upstairs and confer with him." She left the room abruptly.

Fargo looked around. The big wooden desk was

piled with papers, some of them yellowed with age. He picked one up. It was in Spanish, but he could read enough of it to see that it was a land deed. He put it down and moved away from the desk as Faith reentered.

"He asks you to please stay overnight. Perhaps later today or tomorrow he . . ." Faith's voice lost its tone. Fargo wondered what made her so hesitant. "Tomorrow . . . you can deliver your message then."

Fargo nodded. There could be many things worse than spending an afternoon and evening with Faith Lawrence Tate—even if she was married to somebody else. He just hoped the message about his shooting the deputy in Deadwood didn't arrive at the ranch before he left. He felt sure that Faith would believe his side of the story. But would Owen Tate?

It was after noon. Faith suggested they take some refreshment, and she led him through the cool, dark house. Soon they were sitting in a huge dining hall at one end of a long table. Around the table were more than two dozen leather chairs. Red clay jugs stood on the tiled floor. At the far end was a large wooden chair with the Circle T symbol carved in its back.

"Owen used to . . . well, he often invites his hands here for dinner," Faith said. "They call him Il Patrone because he treats them like family. You see, Owen believes that the hands should profit from the ranch too. So he set it up so that they can own their homes, and they get a cut from the year's profits too. Some of the hands are bachelors, but a lot of them have brought their families to live here on the ranch."

"Sounds like a good system," Fargo said, remembering his suspicions about slavery and the sheriff's remarks about the "ranch slaves." He smiled at the thought. Then a door opened and a rotund woman with dark plaited hair bustled in.

"Inez," Faith said to her, "would you bring us some lunch?" The woman nodded and smiled at them then retreated. Faith motioned Fargo to sit down.

Over a meal of tortillas and beef stew they talked about St. Louis and some of the people they had known there. Fargo was amazed how little Faith had changed. She was still graceful and humorous and quick. He remembered how easy it was, and how enjoyable, to find ways to make her laugh.

After coffee they rose and Faith suggested they sit on the ramada to take a siesta. Outside the sun-drenched land was white hot in the sun's glare, but it was cool in the shade of the broad porch. No one was in sight. All the hands were resting after their midday repasts. Faith sat on a woven leather divan and motioned for Fargo to sit beside her. They put their feet up and lay back, eyes closed. Her hand, lying on the divan, touched his lightly.

"Tell me how your husband got this ranch," Fargo said, his eyes still closed.

"He came down twenty years ago," she answered. "Owen's a smart man. Most of the ranchers just squat on the land. But he started tracking down the original owners. Many of them are descendants from the Spanish land grantees. He found them, one by one, and started buying property. He slowly accumulated land. Then, on a trip to Mexico, he came to a small town where the cattle were starving and the people very poor. He bought the herd, and then he decided to invite the people to come along to help out with the ranching. That's how it all started."

Fargo nodded to himself, eyes still closed against the heat, his lean body relaxed and comfortable. He moved his hand to cover hers and felt her grasp his warmly. Fargo opened his eyes. Better to keep an eye out. It wouldn't be a great first impression if Owen Tate just happened to walk onto the ramada and found him napping and holding his wife's hand.

"But now we have trouble," she continued, her eyes closed, but a frown darkening her brow. "You see, there's one piece of land left to buy in the center of the property. Without this property the ranch would be split in two. And it's the land that gives us direct access to the Shawnee Trail. Well, Owen found the owner, and they agreed upon a price. All we have to do is deposit the money in the bank, and they'll transfer the land." She paused.

"That sounds like everything's okay then," Fargo said.

She opened her eyes and turned her face toward him. Her wide eyes were dark with uncertainty. "We've been trying to send the money to the bank for two months. Every time our riders get ambushed and . . . and hanged." Her eyes filled with tears. "We've lost twenty men so far. Now they're all afraid. And we've lost five payments. We're running out of money to buy the land. And the owner is running out of patience. He's threatening to sell to someone else if we can't get the money to him." The tears dripped off her eyelashes and rolled down her cheeks. Fargo let go of her hand and wiped the tears away.

"If we don't get that land," she said, "the ranch will be split. We may lose it all."

"Who do you think is responsible for the hangings?" Fargo asked. "I heard the Spill brothers have been rustling your cattle. Could they be hanging the men and stealing the payments?"

She nodded her head. "That's what I think. That's what everybody thinks. I mean it's the only thing that makes sense. But . . ."

"But what?"

"I don't know how the Spill brothers find out about the payments leaving the ranch. I . . . I have a funny feeling about it all sometimes," Faith said softly. "I feel like it's somebody on the ranch who is involved. I'm scared and I don't know who to trust." Fargo thought of the message from the dying boy. The team is against Il Patrone, he had said. The team is with the sheriff. Well, that could mean that all the ranch hands were against Owen Tate, and they were stealing the money. But it didn't make sense that they would hang each other. And what did the sheriff have to do with it all? Fargo opened his mouth to ask her about Buck Witchell when she spoke again.

"I want to ask you a favor," she said, her eyes holding his. "I'm going to ask Owen if we can hire you to take the payment to the bank in Deadwood. It's not far, half a day's ride. And if anyone can get it there, you can. You can outrun anybody on horseback. We'd pay you anything. Anything you ask." She spoke quickly, hope in her voice. She saw him hesitate. "Oh, please Skye. Please say yes. This is the last of our money. If this doesn't get through, we are finished. Please. Please say yes."

There was a long pause as Fargo looked out to the white heat of the day. In the corral the horses stood in the shade of the stable. The Ovaro had ventured out and loped slowly in a wide circle, glistening black and white in the baking sun.

"I can't, Faith," Fargo said at last. "I can't go into Deadwood because I'm a wanted man."

"Surely that must be a mistake," she said.

"It is," he continued. "One of Buck Witchell's deputies shot at me when I was at the bar. Then he tried to shoot me in the back. But I got him first. It seemed like nobody in the bar, except for Lucia, had seen him draw first. So I could be hanged for murder."

Lucia shook her head and remained silent.

"I can't run and I can't go back to Deadwood," he continued. "I'm heading to Brownwater to find the circuit judge. I figured if I can bring him back and Lucia can testify, I'll get a fair trial and clear my name."

"As long as you're on the Circle T Ranch, you'll be safe," she said. "I promise. The sheriff isn't welcome here." He looked over at her again and saw the worry—this time for him—in her eyes. He had an idea.

"Is there . . . is there a bank in Brownwater?" he asked. "I could take the payment with me."

She shook her head again. "Payment has to be made through the Deadwood bank. We tried that already."

"I'll think about it," he said. "I'd like to help."

"I couldn't ask you to risk your life for this," she said.

Inez appeared and carried a blanket to the side of the broad porch where she proceeded to shake it out.

"Maybe I could talk to your husband now," Fargo said.

"Inez, where is Mr. Tate?" Faith called.

Inez turned slowly and looked at the two of them. Her eyes were dark with thought. "Il Patrone has gone out to ride, Señora," she answered. She turned back, folded the blanket, and went back into the house.

"I'm sorry," Faith said. "Maybe later when he returns."

Fargo wondered how Owen Tate had left. He hadn't heard anyone moving about when they were having lunch. But then it was a large hacienda with thick adobe walls. And they had been sitting on the ramada for an hour and would have seen him if he had gone by. The delay in meeting Owen Tate only increased his curiosity about the mysterious man who moved so quietly around his own ranch, like a ghost.

Faith suddenly stood and stretched. She was as slender as a willow, and his arms ached to hold her again. Fargo rose to his feet as well. The Ovaro was trotting round and round the corral, eager to run free.

"I'd like to take a ride around," he said. "Give my pinto some real exercise." He was eager to be on the open range where his thoughts would straighten themselves out.

A look of fear crossed her face for a brief instant, and he guessed her thoughts. "I'll be back," he said. Relief flooded her face, and he knew he could read Faith Lawrence just as well as he had in the old days. She smiled as if apologizing for her vulnerability and wordlessly retreated into the hacienda.

As he crossed the yard to the stable, he heard a rhythmic ringing sound begin from one of the outbuildings. He turned his steps that way.

One of the adobe buildings on the far side had a

double doorway, wide open to the afternoon breeze. Fargo felt the heat of the forge as he approached. In the dim interior two muscular smithies, stripped to the waist and sweating, bent over their work. One pumped the bellows to keep the red coals glowing while he rotated a long piece of metal that blushed with heat. The other wielded the hammer and brought it down again and again on another piece of fast cooling iron, which he held on an anvil. The noise was deafening. Fargo started to back away when the one with bellows noticed him and motioned him over.

Fargo approached and the smithies paused to show him the irons with the Circle T design they were fashioning for the spring branding. The ranch, one of them explained, was almost self-sufficient. In addition to the blacksmith shop, there was a tannery and saddlemaker, a workshop where women made woolens, and a trading post for the workers. As Fargo left the blacksmiths, they returned to their work.

He had the Ovaro saddled in moments and set off at an easy canter, riding out of the yard and across the grassy plain as the sun sank below the horizon. He rode through the coolness of the evening, galloping aimlessly over the darkening prairie and through the endless chaparral, his thoughts as directionless as his wanderings.

Here and there he sighted the cowpunchers driving small herds of cattle. He knew they were collecting the herd, which had been wandering all winter, in preparation for branding. Several times groups of the punchers approached, pistols drawn to ask him who he was. When he answered, they put their guns away promptly, touched their hats, and rode back to their work. Clearly the word had been circulated that he was a guest on the Circle T. Once he asked if any of them had seen Owen Tate out riding the range, but they said they hadn't recently.

It was night on the land even though the sky still held the daylight. The first stars were twinkling when Fargo decided to head back. It was fully dark by the time he reached the hacienda.

In the stable he lit a lantern and curried the Ovaro for a long time. He still hadn't sorted out his thoughts, he realized. He'd been thinking a lot about Faith. Wondering what kind of man Owen Tate was. Guessing who was responsible for the hangings. Speculating when the Spill brothers gang might try to rustle more cattle. Worrying about whether he would get to Brownwater to find the judge before the sheriff caught up with him. Faith had said he'd be safe on the Circle T. But was he?

Damn, he thought as he brushed the pinto's glossy coat with long strokes. Then there was the message he promised to deliver to Owen Tate. That was the only thing keeping him on the ranch . . . or was it?

He thought of Faith and her familiar golden warmth. He wanted to help her by delivering the land payment. Hell, it wasn't much of a job riding back to Deadwood and making a bank deposit. He had no doubt he could outride anybody who found him on the open range. The Ovaro could outrun any horse he'd ever seen. But the question was what awaited him in Deadwood. Would he be able to slip in, get the money into the bank, and slip away again without running into Buck Witchell? He shook away the thought, realizing he was actually considering it.

But if the payment was so important, why didn't

Owen Tate himself gather a big bunch of his hands and get themselves into town? If he were Tate, he'd made that delivery himself, he thought. Why was Tate sending in his men four by four to get ambushed and hanged? The whole thing didn't add up.

Fargo heard someone walking across the ramada and entering the front door of the hacienda. It sounded like a man. He hurriedly packed away the brushes, blew out the lantern, and went inside.

Inez met him in the front hallway. She was holding a pair of worn boots.

"Are those Mr. Tate's?" Fargo asked.

Inez looked down for an instant, then back at him and smiled. "Sí," she said. "Il Patrone has just come back from riding."

"Where is he?" Fargo asked. "I need to talk to him right now."

"I am sorry, señor," Inez said. "Mr. Tate went upstairs immediately. He is very tired, and he left me instructions he does not want to be disturbed. Perhaps you can see him in the morning. Or talk to Mrs. Tate. She has gone upstairs as well, but she rises early in the morning."

Fargo nodded.

Inez offered him some cold meat, tortillas, and beer for supper and then led him to his room, large comfortable quarters at the back of the house on the ground floor. She brought in an oil lamp, fresh water for the pitcher, and a few extra blankets and told him to ring the bell on the wall if he needed anything.

When she had gone, Fargo lay down on the bed and looked up at the thick wooden beamed ceiling. His curiosity burned about Owen Tate. Everyone he had met on the ranch seemed to revere Tate as some kind of saint. But in Deadwood he was seen as a land-grabbing bastard. What was the truth? If only he could catch sight of him, have a few words with him, know what kind of man he was.

Fargo heard a creak in the floorboards overhead. Damn it, he would, he decided. He silently rose and blew out the lamp, then took his boots off. Unlatching the window, he swung it silently outward and eased his lean body out onto the ramada. He quickly crossed it in his bare feet and stepped out into the yard. It would be an easy matter to climb up onto the low roof of the porch, which ran all the way around the adobe building. And once he climbed up the sloping tile roof, he could look into any of the windows on the second floor. The one just above him was lit.

Fargo silently climbed up the support beam and hoisted himself onto the roof. As he crawled forward, a loose tile slipped and clattered down the roof, falling off the edge and into the yard with a muffled thud. Fargo froze and shrank down onto the roof, watching the lighted window above him. He waited for several minutes. No one appeared. He began to edge forward again, very slowly, feeling carefully for any other loose tiles and avoiding them.

Then he heard her voice, muffled by the closed window. She was speaking, then pausing, then speaking again. The sound was rhythmic. He strained his ears to make out the words, but her voice was too faint. Owen Tate wasn't making a sound. Fargo had reached the wall under the window and slowly, slowly, he eased himself up so that he could look over the sill into the lighted room.

There, in the wide carved wooden bed, lay Faith, a book held before her. Fargo realized what he had been hearing. She was reading poetry aloud to herself. Owen Tate was nowhere to be seen. Fargo shifted his knees so that he balanced comfortably— or as comfortably as one could on a cold, raked tiled roof—and waited. Five, ten minutes passed. Owen Tate would be sure to come in. Finally Faith put a marker in the book, laid it on a table, and blew out the lamp.

So, Fargo thought. She and Owen slept in separate rooms. Perhaps that was some of the sadness he heard in her voice when she spoke about her husband.

So Tate would be sleeping in another room, per- haps around the other side of the hacienda. Fargo silently made his way along the top of the roof, turning the first corner, then the second, then the third. None of the other windows on the second floor were lit. Tate, like his wife, had already gone to sleep.

When Fargo reached Faith's window again, he quietly slid down the roof. He quickly looked about the yard, which remained deserted, then he dropped to the ground. He stooped to pick up the roof tile that lay in the dirt and slid it under the wooden steps of the ramada where it wouldn't be found. No need to arouse any suspicions. In an- other minute he had eased himself through the win- dow, undressed, and lay in his bed.

He hadn't seen Owen Tate. And the only thing he had learned about the man was that he didn't sleep with his wife. Not very helpful. But intriguing, he thought as sleep enveloped him. It was a trou- bled sleep full of dreams of hangings, faceless men, and questions.

The dawn light was just coming in his window when Fargo awoke. He splashed water on his face and dressed quickly, determined not to miss Owen Tate.

He walked down the long hallway, heard a clatter in the kitchen, and smelled coffee. The door to Tate's study stood ajar. Fargo pushed it gently, and it silently swung open. An oil lamp flickered on the desk, augmenting the pale light that came in through the broad wooden casements overlooking the yard.

No one was in the study. Fargo approached the desk. The leather chair still held the imprint of Tate's body, and Fargo put his hand on the leather seat. Still warm. He glanced at the papers and saw that Tate had been working on the ranch's accounts. Even a cursory look showed him that the positive balance was decreasing while the debts were mounting.

He picked up a carved silver item from the desk and inspected it, realizing it was Tate's seal with the Circle T imprint on the bottom. A pile of bills and documents had been stamped and initialed with a bold "O.T." Footsteps approached and he looked up as Faith entered the room.

"Good morning, Skye," she said with a warm smile. "Sleep well?"

"Very," he lied. "I was hoping to see Mr. Tate this morning. I see he was just in here."

"Oh," she said, her eyes darkening for an instant, then clearing. "Yes. He was working at his desk quite early this morning. He just rode out. But he'll be back in later. He . . . he knows about your message. I've told him how important it is for you to see him."

Fargo nodded and placed Tate's seal back on the desk. He felt a flash of anger rise in him. Goddamn it, he thought. If a stranger came with an urgent message from a dying man, I'd sure as hell give him five minutes. What could be keeping Tate so busy? Or was he avoiding Fargo purposefully?

He followed Faith into the dining room where Inez served them breakfast, eaten mostly in silence. She could read him as well as he could her. She could see he was angry at not meeting Tate yet. But she was pretending not to notice.

"How about a ride?" she suggested, rising. "I'm going out to look over the herd. I try to get out there every day, to keep up the morale of our cowpunchers."

"Maybe we'll run into your husband," Fargo said as he got to his feet.

"Maybe," she said.

Faith disappeared upstairs to change into riding clothes, and Fargo went to the corral to see to the horses. Around the corner of the stable a man in sombrero napped in the morning sun and woke at his approach. While Fargo saddled his pinto, Faith's pure white stallion was saddled with a honey-leather ladies' sidesaddle with its three asymmetrical horns. Someone had curried the Ovaro carefully Fargo noted as he smoothed out the saddle blanket. All of the horses were well tended here.

Fargo led the two saddled mounts into the yard as Faith came out of the hacienda. She had changed into a white leather riding skirt and fringed jacket. Her golden hair was hidden under a tawny wide-brimmed hat. As she swung up onto her stallion, Fargo admired her willowy figure and the lightness of her long legs. She sat well on her horse he noticed as they cantered out of the gate and onto the open range. She sat tall and moved easily with the horse, her slenderness yielding to the stallion's motions as tall grass to the blowing wind. Owen Tate was a lucky man, Fargo thought again.

The day was already heating up by the time they reached the broad grasslands that lay to the south. The rolling hills, verdant with spring, were broken only by streams and stands of cottonwoods and live oak. As they rode, he saw more of the cowpokes herding small groups of straying cattle off in the distance. By noontime they stopped at a wooded creek to water the horses. They had ridden for hours, scarcely saying a word.

Fargo filled his canteen and handed it to Faith, who sat on the grassy bank. He watched as she tilted her head back. Her throat, as slender and smooth as a doe's, contracted as she swallowed. When she finished, she handed up the canteen, removed her hat, and shook out her shining hair. From the angle he stood above her, he saw the sweet curve of one breast through the blouse, which was unbuttoned at the neck.

He lowered himself to sit beside her.

"Skye," she said. "I don't know how to tell you this, but your coming here to the ranch . . ."

He laid a finger across her mouth. He knew exactly what she would say and how she would say it. That was always how it had between the two of them.

She parted her lips and took his finger into her mouth, caressing it with her tongue. And then he seized her.

6

Fargo's mouth was on hers in an instant. Her hands slid up his back and clutched him as they rolled together, over and over down the bank, halting on the grass just next to the rippling creek. His tongue plunged into her sweet familiar mouth, and she held him close as though afraid to let go, moaning deep in her throat as his fingers combed through her long blond hair.

He felt her soft breasts against his chest and her frightened panting. Her long legs parted, and she wrapped them around him as he pushed his hips against hers, feeling the electric shock when his hardness met her firm mound despite the clothing in between. He pumped again against her as she responded, her hips making the subtle movements against him that he knew so well.

They parted, gasping for breath.

"Oh, Skye," she said, her eyes filled with tears. "I wanted you again the moment you walked into the hacienda. Please, darling." He stopped her words with his mouth. He drank her kisses, hungry for more of her. Her hand came up to her blouse, and he felt her try to unbutton it, fumbling, then impatiently she pulled at the neck and he heard the buttons give way as her blouse opened. He kissed downward, along the arching curve of her long neck, across the smoothness of her shoulder, slipping the lacy camisole down to reveal her white and pink breast, round, the nipple erect. How well he remembered her. He took the nipple into his mouth as his hand caressed down the side of her narrow hip to the hem of her skirt, which he pulled upward.

"Yes, yes," she breathed, her fingers entwined in his hair and tickling his ears. He remembered the sensitive spot behind her knees that made her giggle and then explored further, trailing up her bloomer-clad thigh, making her shiver. Finally his fingers came to the top of her bloomers and edged inside, across her smooth belly. He felt the tickle of fur, and he slipped his hand further to find her moist folded wetness.

They could hold back no more. He buried his face against her breasts and felt her bite his shoulder as he pulled down her bloomers. She furiously undid his jeans, grasping his huge hardness, squeezing him as she sucked on his tongue, breathing hard, pulling him toward her. He raised himself above her, struggling out of his jeans as she kicked her bloomers off from around her ankles, and then he plunged into her, hard, deep, as she cried out.

Again, again, he thrust into her as she bucked against him, writhing in pleasure, her hands clawing his back.

"Yes, yes, my darling, please, give me all of it, all of it," she moaned.

She was as sweet as memory, as familiar as his own body, he thought as he closed his eyes and felt her under him. He plunged deep into her tight hotness, heard her gasp again. He kissed her, drinking deep as he felt the passion gathering in her. She began the quaking he remembered, shivering and tensing as she pushed her hips against his, tighter and tighter as her moans increased in intensity.

"Yes, yes, oh God . . ." she said. And he let himself go, exploding into her, pumping without being able to stop as she cried out and clutched him, knowing she was feeling what he was, knowing he was giving her the same waves of ecstasy, knowing that at this moment, once again, they had come together. They had relived their time together, brought back the past as the green grass and blue sky whirled around them.

Fargo opened his eyes. Through the cottonwood branches he saw a few clouds floating above them. He glanced over at Faith, who lay with her eyes closed, her head on his arm. Her hair billowed around her, golden against the tender blades of grass, her pale skin almost transparent in the dappled shade. Fargo plucked a blade of grass with the other hand and tickled her soft nipple. She stirred and smiled, opening her eyes. The nipple hardened to a point, and she snuggled closer to him, guiding his hand downward to her swollen wetness.

He felt himself ready again, eager to be inside her. He eased himself over and gently slid in, moving very slowly, looking down at her as he moved. Her long smooth legs came up to wrap around him, and he eased even more deeply into her as he felt her breathing quicken. He continued to look into her hazel eyes, noticing the flecks of gold and how familiar her every expression was to him. She reached up and pulled him down, opening her mouth to take in his tongue as she began to move under him just as slowly, and he felt them both building again, holding back, slowing, plunging deeper into her tightness, until he heard her panting, her eyes wide. The tightness gathered at the base of him and, as he felt her contractions and heard her gasp, he slowly, slowly pushed all the way inside her, spurting into her, all of himself, again and again and again.

After a few moments he rolled away, and they lay on the grass, fingers entwined, until their panting had subsided.

"How about a cold bath?" he asked. She grinned and rose, sliding down the bank and wading out into the stream with a shriek. They splashed each other for a time, then dried off with Fargo's shirt. He fetched a fresh one from the saddlebag as they got half dressed. Then Faith brought some food from her pack, and they ate in the shade, lounging on the grass and talking about old times.

He wondered if she would say anything about Owen Tate, but she never did. She had said Tate was a wonderful man, so did she feel guilty about what was happening between them? It wasn't like Faith to be dishonest with anyone. He knew that. On the other hand, if Owen wasn't sleeping with her anymore, maybe they had an understanding. He wouldn't ask. He would have to wait for her to bring it up.

It was late afternoon when they finished eating and had just stood to finish getting dressed. Faith was buttoning up her blouse, and Fargo pulling on his boots when a rider appeared on the hillside. He was heading straight for them. Fargo reached for his Colt, but then his keen sight recognized the rider and he relaxed. It was Hank.

He galloped toward them on his bay, reining in at the last moment and dismounting. Hank gave them a suspicious stare. Faith's cheeks were flushed, her hair mussed, and she was just buttoning her top button, one of the few left on her blouse. Fargo calmly continued pulling on his boots. It would have been clear to an idiot what had been going on, Fargo thought. And Hank was no fool.

"What the hell?" Hank muttered, and a long silence followed.

"What is it, Hank?" Faith asked, her voice betraying nothing.

"Miz Tate," he said pointedly. "Some of the boys saw you go this way and wanted me to find you. They've got most of the herd gathered over to the west and wondered if you wanted to come see."

"Of course, Hank," Faith said. "That's why we're out riding this afternoon. We were heading that way."

Hank shot an angry look at Skye and stalked back to his bay. He mounted and sped off without a backward glance. Great, Fargo thought. Hank hadn't liked him from the first moment they met. He'd been convinced that Fargo not only knew something about the hangings but was responsible. Now Hank knew that Fargo had dallied with the boss's wife. Fargo was certain Hank would use the information to no good end. He decided he should say something to Faith about his suspicions.

"I gather Hank suspects what's going on," Fargo said.

"So?" Faith said, defiantly. "It's none of his business. Hank works for me."

"And for your husband," Fargo pointed out. "I think Hank will tell Owen what he suspects."

"Look, Skye," Faith said, turning toward him. "Owen would understand . . . I . . . I will tell you everything tonight when we're back at the hacienda. It's a long story. But then you'll understand too."

She reached up and pulled him down toward him, kissing him gently. He smiled.

"I can't argue with you, Faith," he said. "I never could."

They mounted and rode out, heading west. The sun had lost its white midday glare and turned golden as it sank toward the horizon, and a dry, hot wind puffed across the chaparral. The warm lowering light threw their galloping shadows across the woolly plain as they rode.

Suddenly Faith glanced over at Skye with a big smile, gave a yell, and urged her horse forward in a race. Fargo lightly dug his knees into the sides of the pinto. The Ovaro, happy to be running again, moved ahead joyfully beneath him, its strong legs seemingly tireless as the ground flashed by beneath them. He galloped up next to Faith and her stallion and pulled ahead. One length, five, ten, a quarter mile. Fargo glanced back over his shoulder as he galloped. Faith's stallion was light-footed but without the stamina of the pinto. After a few miles Fargo slowed a little, and the Ovaro reluctantly obeyed as the stallion caught up with them again. Faith was laughing, her hat blown back from the wind, her hair a golden tangle around her face.

"You win!" she gasped.

They splashed through a creek crossing. Across the stream bed, on a gentle hillside, Fargo sighted a few straggling cattle in clusters. Some cowpunchers appeared and swooped down to round them up and drive them back over the hill. Faith waved to them, and they hallooed back. They could hear the low moaning of a herd nearby. They trotted up the hill, which was bathed in the reddening light of the sunset. At the top of the rise they paused side by side and looked down over a roiling sea of darkness.

The cattle were milling on the grassy bottom of the wide valley below them, where night was gathering. Thousands of head of cattle. Yes, Owen Tate was a very lucky and very wealthy man.

All around the edges of the herd cowpunchers rode to and fro like bees swarming around a dark pool of molasses. As they watched, two punchers appeared far to the east, driving twenty cows and calves before them, which joined the main herd. Several more appeared from the south, driving several beeves.

"We've called in most of the line riders from the periphery to help gather the herd for the spring branding," Faith explained. "That's tomorrow. Our hands are so good, some of them can cut and brand as many as six hundred calves in a single day."

Fargo smiled at the obvious pride in her voice.

"Then they'll cut the herd for the ones to be taken up the Shawnee to market," she continued. "The rest we'll leave here to make some more calves before next year's drive." Her voice changed. "We've lost so much money on these stolen land payments that I've . . . well, Owen has told them to take most of the cattle up to market this year. We need the money. We can't afford to lose much more and still keep the ranch going and pay all the hands."

Fargo gazed across the noisy herd. They were milling, moving aimlessly, settling down for the night. The light was still in the western sky, but in the east, the first stars had appeared and darkness clung to the ground. Far on the other side a golden flicker of a campfire appeared, a mile or so distant.

"Let's drop in on them," Faith suggested.

They galloped down the hillside, then angled off, giving the herd wide berth. The cattle were just beginning to go to their knees, one by one. With luck—and no lightning storm, no sudden noise, no wandering coyotes—the herd would remain quiet all night. But if any one of those or a thousand other unpredictable accidents occurred, the thousands of head of cattle could leap to their feet in an instant and stampede madly into the night. That was a cowpoke's worst, and most often-realized, fear. All he could do was ride after them, try to turn them, try to keep them from running themselves to exhaustion or into ravines. And, if the herd scattered, it could take days or weeks to round them all up again.

Knowing all this, Faith and Skye were careful not to ride too close to the herd. Although the cattle seemed calm now, a horse faltering or any sudden movement could get it started. No need to tempt fate.

The night riders were already on duty, four of the punchers who rode continually around the herd, two clockwise and two in the opposite direction, spaced far apart. In this way the herd was as well guarded as it could be without a fence. The punchers would spell each other throughout the long night, taking turns in shifts. As they passed one of the riders in the distance, Fargo heard him singing, but whether it was to himself or the cows was impossible to say.

Fargo and Faith rounded the southern edge of the herd and started up the far slope. Fargo could see the campfire clearly now, the chuckwagon drawn up close, lip down, the punchers lined up with their tin plates for the evening's meal.

All of them looked up as they reined in. "Welcome, Miz Tate," one of them said stepping forward. Fargo recognized Curly, who had been at the line camp. Juan was there also, and he recognized a few of the faces of the other men from the north line camp.

"Where's Hank?" Faith asked, looking around.

"He's gone back up north to check up on the rest of the boys," Curly said. "He'll be back tomorrow morning for the branding. How about some grub? I mean, would you like some dinner, Miz Tate?"

Faith smiled and took a seat on a log near the fire. Juan brought her a plate of beef and a fork that he tried to polish secretively on his vest before handing it to her. Fargo took a plate and found a seat a little ways away. The punchers took their seats and ate in silence.

"How does the herd look this year?" Faith asked at last to break the silence. Several of the punchers were quick to answer her, but Juan won out.

"They've made us a lot of sturdy calves this winter, Señora," he said. "And Il Patrone was right about those cross-breeds. They are very strong and many, many pounds of beef." He slapped his chest and his thigh to explain what he meant. "Only Il Patrone would think to make these Texas bulls marry these Eastern reds. Very smart."

Faith laughed, and the other punchers nodded assent.

"Yes, Owen does know what he's doing with cattle," she said. "Did he . . . did he ride by this way tonight?" she asked.

Several of the men looked about hopefully.

"Il Patrone? Coming out this way?" one muttered. They shook their heads.

"Well," Faith said lightly, "I guess he rode in another direction. I'll tell him how good a job you're doing when I get back home." The punchers grinned.

"I haven't seen Il Patrone since last autumn," Curly said. "He used to come out here all the time with us."

"I know," Faith said. Fargo heard the veil in her voice. "It has been a hard winter. He's been working on that land deal, you know."

"Seems like ever since he started that, us punchers have been paying the price," one voice muttered. There was a deep silence, and several of the punchers shifted uncomfortably. Fargo tried to see which one had said it, but it was too dusky. Faith had heard it too.

"It does seem like that," she said with a sigh. "I know you all think there's a curse on this ranch. I've heard that too." Her voice brightened. "But as soon as we can catch those Spill brothers or whoever is causing this trouble, we can get that payment delivered. Then the ranch will be safe again. Owen Tate would never let you boys down."

"Here's to Il Patrone," Curly said, raising his tin mug high. Everybody else followed suit, and Faith caught Fargo's eye and smiled. The smile was sad, secretly sad.

Then one of the punchers brought out a harmonica and played it as a gigantic pumpkin-colored moon peered over the horizon. It rose as the cowpokes sang some songs and Faith joined in. The moon turned golden, then frigid white as the night wind turned cold.

"We'd best be getting back," Faith said finally.

"It's almost time for the second shift," Curly said.

Fargo and Faith remounted and headed south in order to circle the herd. In the silvery moonlight the sleeping herd looked like a dark bumpy rug spread out on the grass. They were halfway around when Fargo reined in and looked into the darkness. Faith noticed and paused also.

"What is it?" she asked, her voice low. Far off they heard the long howl of a coyote which was repeated. But it was not the noise that had stopped Fargo. He continued to peer at the herd as the seconds passed. A minute. Two. Three. Yes, now he was certain. There were no night riders circling the herd. The cattle lay unwatched on the plain.

"No riders," he whispered back. "Come on."

They rode nearer, at a slow walk. Still nothing moved.

Then, suddenly, Fargo heard the sound he feared. From the far side of the sleeping herd a soft popping sound. Gunshots—five, six times.

In an instant the cattle were awake and up on their feet, confused. The cows nearest the firing on the north side had turned to run from the sound. Those closest to Fargo and Faith turned all at once and began running blindly, a wide wall of stampeding cattle heading straight for them.

"Ride!" Fargo shouted as Faith stared wide-eyed at the oncoming herd. She shook herself and spurred the white stallion, which came around instantly into a gallop. The stallion and the pinto headed away from the cattle, running in the same direction, just a few hundred feet in front of the stampede.

Fargo glanced back at the oncoming cattle, measuring the distance to either side. They could do no good this far out in front. And first he had to get Faith out of harm's way.

He shouted to her, but she didn't hear him above the bellowing of the cattle and the thunder of their pounding hooves. He turned the pinto toward her stallion until they galloped close and she looked over, her eyes wide with fear. He motioned her to follow him and gradually eased the pinto toward the left side of the herd. He glanced back from time to time as they slowly made progress cutting across the path of the cattle until they rode off to one side of the stampede. Fargo drew in the pinto and watched as the dark mass thundered by.

"Oh hell!" Faith screamed above the din. Fargo nodded. She was feeling rage as well as fear for the future of the ranch—the hangings, their money for the land stolen, now this.

But right now Fargo was more curious about who had been firing the shots than he was interested in cursing fate. In the silver moonlight he spotted four dark figures on horseback galloping along with the cattle. Skye drew the Sharps rifle from its saddle sheath.

For a moment he thought they might be ranch hands. But then he saw the tall shape of their dark hats—rustlers. He knew immediately it was the Spill brothers gang. Nobody else would dare to rustle a herd this big with this many cowpunchers in the immediate vicinity. Fargo wondered how many rustlers there were. He could see four of them coming. And there was one of him. And Faith. The riders spotted them too, he saw. They swerved away from them, plunging deeper into the herd. They didn't want a fight; they wanted the cattle. But he wanted Faith as far away from the rustlers as possible.

"Get going! Up the hill!" he shouted to her above the noise. "Circle back to the camp!" Chances were she could find some of her cowpunchers up that way, he thought. And he'd watch that these four went on by. Then he'd follow her to make sure she got back to the camp safely. Faith spurred her stallion and headed up the hill as he turned his attention back toward the four.

Just then he saw the glint of moonlight on steel from one of the four, and he tensed as a rifle exploded. He ducked as the shot zinged by him. So they *did* want a fight after all.

"Goddamn rustlers," he muttered as he instantly raised his Sharps to return the fire. He took slow aim and fired. The man was jolted out of his saddle as the shot hit him, and the body slid off the saddle and disappeared beneath the pounding hooves. The other three had drawn their rifles, Fargo saw. He took aim at one and squeezed off another shot. The man's hat flew off his head and, even in the darkness, Fargo could see the gaping blackness where his face had been a moment before. The impact carried the man's body backward off his saddle. The other two were almost even with him now, hunched down on their mounts, trying to get a good shot at him.

Another bullet whizzed by, but wide of him. Fargo raised the Sharps again and blasted a third man out of his saddle. The shot caught him in the side and threw him off into the bawling, stampeding cattle. Several of the cattle had broken away from the main body of the herd and were running wildly toward him. Fargo spurred the Ovaro, which came around and began galloping in the same direction as the approaching cattle. Fargo raised his Sharps once more, aiming at the remaining rustler now riding ahead of him among the cattle.

Above the noise of the pounding hooves his keen hearing detected a thin piercing scream. It was his name, or did he imagine that? He whirled about, looking back toward the sound. There on the hillside he saw a white horse surrounded by dark moving shadows, men on horseback. Faith! They had her! He cursed the rustlers and started to rein in the pinto to turn back.

But just then he glanced back at the remaining horseman he had been pursuing and saw a flash of yellow and then an explosion of sound and pain erupted, hot fire in his left shoulder. Everything happened in slow motion. Only his thoughts moved quickly.

The impact of the bullet tore him out of the saddle and ripped the reins from his hand. He flailed at the saddle, knowing he must not fall under the cruel hooves of the stampeding cattle. He tried to grasp the saddle horn, but his left side was paralyzed, and he was unbalanced. He felt himself slipping off sideways. Just as he plummeted, he slipped the pointed toe of his boot out of the stirrup so that he would make a clean fall to earth and the galloping Ovaro would not drag his body over the plains.

7

Fargo was jolted as his wounded shoulder hit the hard ground first. He tucked his arms and legs into a ball and rolled, expecting any moment to feel the heavy hooves of cattle strike him. The noise was deafening.

He rolled, once, twice and then gathered his feet under him and stood. He turned to face the stampede. Cows and bulls and calves bellowed, rushing blindly forward on all sides. One headed his way, then swerved at the last instant, brushing by him, almost knocking him off his feet. Mercifully his shoulder was still numb. It wouldn't stay that way, he knew. No time even to glance at it now.

The cattle weren't as packed together as they had been when the stampede began. He quickly found that he could dodge them, calculating the spaces between them as they rushed toward him. He'd be all right if one didn't change its mind at the last instant and gore him, he thought as he jumped aside, barely avoiding a massive longhorn.

Fargo glanced over to the nearby hillside, calculating the distance he would have to negotiate to get out of the stampede. He began to make a few steps in that direction as he continued to dodge the rushing cattle. Then suddenly he heard a high whinny. He glanced to the hillside and saw his pinto running free of the stampede, galloping upstream of the cattle.

He spat out dust and wet his lips. Then he whistled, hoping the sound would cut through the bellowing and thunder of the running herd. The Ovaro swerved immediately, entering the stampede as though it was swimming a current, heading toward him. Fargo continued to jump and dodge as the cattle ran, favoring his right side. He felt the numbness in his shoulder spreading. Then the trusty pinto was beside him and, using his right hand only, he leapt onto its back, patting its neck gratefully.

As the pinto galloped with the herd, edging out of the stampede, Fargo's keen eyes swept the land around him. On the far edges of the herd he saw some mounted figures—cowpokes or more rustlers, he couldn't be sure. Faith and the group of dark horsemen were nowhere in sight.

Fargo was now clear of the cattle. He urged the pinto up the slope toward the campfire. He would need help. In the distance he saw the red embers, but no movement. There were figures lying on the ground.

He jumped down to investigate. The first body, one of the Mexican cowpokes, lay in a pool of blood. The second had no wound he could see. He put his right hand on the man's chest and felt a heartbeat. Out cold, he decided. Several of the other punchers had been shot. Then he heard a groan.

One of the cowboys moved, and Fargo hastened over. It was Curly, who sat up slowly, rubbing his head.

"What happ . . . shit!" Curly said, seeing Fargo standing before him in the light of the dying fire.

Fargo glanced down for the first time and saw his

own blood-soaked shirt. He tentatively explored the wound with his right hand. One hole in the front and one in back. The bullet had gone clean through the shoulder. He wiggled the fingers of his left hand, feeling the first shooting pain. Clean through the muscle. No bone shattered. Just a lot of blood.

"It's nothing," Fargo said. "We got bigger problems."

Curly looked around in confusion and then horror as he continued to rub the back of his neck. From the valley below Fargo heard the sounds of the stampede, distant now. That goddamn Spill brothers gang had made off with the entire herd.

"Guess they cold-cocked you," Fargo said. "They killed some of the rest. And they must have jumped your night riders too. The whole herd is heading to Mexico."

Curly swore. And then swore again as he rose and inspected the bodies—four dead, the rest unconscious. They heard a movement. Fargo and Curly crouched and drew at once, pointing in the direction of the noise. But it was Juan, coming to.

As Fargo told them what he had seen, he fashioned a sling for his left arm out of a plaid shirt from one of the dead men. The bleeding had just about stopped, but any motion would start it up again, he knew. The throbbing had just begun. And, from experience, Fargo knew it would intensify soon. It was going to be a long night.

"We've got to go after those rustlers right now," he concluded.

"Just the three of us?" said Curly, gulping.

"They won't expect pursuit this soon," Fargo said. "We'll surprise them. It'll be our only advantage."

"Sí, sí," Juan said.

"Besides, they have Faith . . . Mrs. Tate," Fargo added.

"Let's go," Curly said immediately, anger in his voice. Juan nodded, his dark face grim.

Most of the remuda had been run off by the rustlers, but a few of the horses had escaped and wandered back toward the campfire. Curly and Juan caught a couple of the strongest ones and mounted. Fargo sat on the pinto and awkwardly reloaded his Colt and Sharps. Without the use of his left hand, he had to hold the weapons under his arm. The throbbing grew stronger. He gritted his teeth and thought of Faith, and the anger welled up in him, obliterating everything else—the pain, the risk, the danger.

After a last check of the other cowpokes, none of whom seemed close to consciousness, the three of them galloped down the hillside.

Tracking a stampeding herd, even in the dark of night, was as simple as following a wide road. They galloped hard for more than two hours, fording the Rio Grande and entering Mexico. The land became more rugged, cut by dry ravines. The rustlers were guiding the herd, Fargo saw as they followed the trail that angled westward. The Spill gang could sure handle cattle well, he thought. They had run across only a few groups of stragglers, which meant the rustlers had firm control over the herd.

The gang had a good half hour start on them, but the three of them could ride faster than the cattle would run, Fargo realized. And after a while the cattle would calm down naturally and slow their pace. Then, no matter what the Spill brothers did, short of starting another stampede, the herd would move at the pace it wanted—usually a slow, creaking, steady gait.

They should be catching up to them, Fargo thought. He slowed the Ovaro and signaled the others to hold back. They fell into a walk, Fargo straining his ears to hear any sounds in the still night.

They had just reached a creek when the pain in Fargo's shoulder redoubled. A hot flush crept along his skin around the wound. He reined in and dismounted, leading the Ovaro to drink. Juan and Curly followed suit.

Fargo knelt by the water and drank long. Then he plunged his hand into the water, feeling along the bottom, until he encountered a cool, smooth band of silt. Well, it was better than nothing, he thought. He pulled his right hand out of the water, tore away his shirt from around the bullet wound, and packed it with the cool silt. The hot flush went away immediately, as did the pain. He knew it wouldn't last, but he was grateful for the momentary relief. He took another drink, then stood and remounted. The three of them rode slowly now.

Fargo peered at the earth beneath them, dimpled by the heavy hooves of the Circle T herd. The cattle were walking now. The men would have to go very slowly forward, lest they suddenly find themselves in the middle of the rustlers' encampment.

Then he heard it ahead—the lowing and the noisy creak and thud of the herd on the move. His keen hearing also picked up the two-note coo-c-o-o of a burrowing owl straight ahead of them. The little sand-colored birds lived in prairie dog burrows; their call was seldom so loud. Then he heard the call again, ahead and off to the right. And again from the other direction. He realized it was a signal. The rustlers were signaling each other. He hoped it wasn't an alarm. In that case they had been sighted.

They came up to the top of a rise and paused. Below them lay a wide, dry valley, bordered by low sandy bluffs. The herd darkened the broad floor. Fargo's sharp eyes picked out four riders circling the herd, two in each direction, just as the cowpunchers had been doing before they were jumped. Fargo smiled to himself.

All right, he thought. Maybe we can beat the Spill brothers at their own game. Then, on the far side of the valley, he spotted a dim golden glimmer of light that winked out immediately. He continued to stare at the spot, and the light winked on again. Fargo felt absolutely certain that when he got over there, he would find Faith and the rest of the Spill brothers gang.

He watched for another moment and heard the call of the burrowing owl again. Yes, that was the signal. The all-clear. He exchanged looks with Curly and Juan, and the three of them backed down the hillside. Fargo headed toward a ravine they had passed, which lay like a dark gash in the slope. It was surrounded by sage brush. They tethered their mounts there, out of sight.

Fargo swiftly outlined his plan, then untied the coil of rope from his saddle and hoisted it over his good shoulder. Curly and Juan took their ropes as well. They made their way on foot over the hill.

They took a long time descending into the valley in full view of the night riders circling the herd. They had to take advantage of every inch of cover—rock, ravine, or sagebrush. Fargo watched the two cowpunchers carefully. The three of them didn't have much of a chance against the gang of rustlers. But he could increase their chances if he had an idea of how these men could move, think, and act under pressure. And he wasn't disappointed. He was impressed to see how the two punchers advanced, silently and carefully. By the time they all reached the bottom of the hill, Fargo had decided that if he had only two men to help him, he was glad it happened to be these two. At least something was going right.

The three men crouched behind a thicket of sage. One of the night riders galloped by in one direction. Two minutes later another came. Then about five minutes later the other two rode by. Again Fargo heard the owl call. The riders seemed to make it each time they completed a circle. Not far from them, the herd was sleeping. Across from them, not far from the cattle, was a huge log. Fargo measured the open space before them. It just might work. Or it might fail miserably.

Two riders had just swept by when Fargo sent Curly scurrying across the open space with one end of the rope. At Fargo's instructions Curly had already secured the other end to a large rock next to them. Fargo inwardly cursed the wound in his shoulder that made his left hand useless. He wiggled the fingers and, feeling the pain shoot through his arm, decided not to try it again. The effect of the silt was wearing off, and the throbbing began again in earnest.

Fargo watched as the rope stretched across the open space in the darkness. Curly had the other end tied now. The long line was taut, a good foot off the ground. He and Juan crouched, waiting in the darkness, ears straining for the sound of hoofbeats.

A minute later he heard them. The rider approached from the left. He tensed. If the rider shot his gun, their plan could fail. The horse came into view, cantering easily, approaching the rope, which was hidden by the darkness.

The horse hit the rope and pitched forward with a high shriek, throwing the rider over its head. The rustler vaulted through the air and then landed heavily with a crack. Juan and Fargo jumped out of the bush and raced forward. The rustler remained still. Probably broke his neck, Fargo thought, as he grabbed the bridle of the frightened horse and led it quickly away, tying it behind the bush. They had just crouched again, when they heard the hoofbeats of the second rider coming from the right. Again the ambush went off perfectly. This time the rider did not break his neck when he was thrown, but Curly knocked him cold as he came to his feet. Once again they secured the horse, dragged away the body, and waited for round two.

Fargo heard the sound of the burrowing owl, and he whistled back twice. All was silent.

After another five minutes had passed, Fargo heard hoofbeats approaching again. On the left? He listened again. No, on the right. The riders had gotten off their timing, and they would both arrive at the same time. Hell, this was going to be tight.

The sounds grew louder, and the riders came into view, one in each direction, both heading for the rope stretched across the path.

Fargo measured the distance to each rider. It looked as if one would reach the rope well before the other. That could mean trouble. He tensed himself, drawing his Colt out of its holster, ready to rush forward. They would try not to fire if possible. Gunfire would alert the rest of the gang up on the hillside, and it might start another stampede.

The first rider hit the rope, and the horse pitched

forward. Fargo heard the snap of the horse's leg and its agonized scream. The second rider, coming full speed, reined in to avoid hitting the first horse, but he was coming too fast, and the rope caught and he went over as well.

Fargo and Juan rushed forward. One rustler lay still. The second had rolled immediately to his feet and stood in a tense crouch, his gun drawn. As soon as he sighted Fargo and Juan rushing toward him, he fired. Fargo leaped aside as the bullet split the air where he had been. Just then Curly, who had crept up behind the rustler, brought his pistol butt down on the man's head. The man dropped to his knees and then sprawled in the dust.

At the sound of the shot a few of the cattle nearest them came to their feet and stood, moving their heads from side to side. But there was no panic among the herd. After running for a few hours, the herd was too tired to stampede again.

"Check that one," Fargo said, pointing at the rustler who had been knocked out by his fall. "Make damn sure he's out cold. That gunshot will bring the rest of them down on us in an instant."

Fargo glanced up where he had seen the light flicker before. He saw a sudden brightness, a golden spot on the hillside, like a door opened and a figure moving against the brightness.

Then, from across the valley, he heard the call of a screech owl, a series of low-pitched whistles. Fargo thought quickly. Should he repeat the screech owl call? Or was that asking if everything was all right? After a moment's hesitation he whistled like the burrow owl, the sound the men had used as they galloped around the herd. After a few seconds he repeated it. And then repeated it twice more. He hoped whoever was listening didn't wonder why the answers were all coming from the same place. The golden glow on the hillside winked out and all was still.

Well, his whistle had either just told the Spill brothers that all was well, or alerted them to an imminent attack. They'd find out soon enough which it was.

The horse with the broken leg lay panting on the ground, struggling to rise. Juan pulled a knife and slit its throat. Then they tied up and gagged the three unconscious rustlers. The fourth had indeed broken his neck.

"Good plan," Juan said as they finished and prepared to move on.

"Good execution," Fargo said. "You fellows are right handy. Let's hope it continues to go this well."

They moved off, skirting the sleeping herd. When they had reached the bottom of the hill, Fargo asked if either of them could whistle like an owl.

"I used to be pretty good," Curly said. "I think I could."

Fargo and Juan left Curly at the bottom of the hill with instructions to answer the rustler's all-clear signal if he heard it from above, and to come immediately when the shooting began.

Juan and Fargo crept up the hillside, dodging from rock to bush, heading toward the glimmer of light. When they had almost reached the top, they heard voices. They eased forward silently until they stood behind a stand of sage.

Ten feet away two men stood talking beside a string of tethered horses, Faith's white stallion among them. The rustlers' backs were toward Fargo and Juan. A silent look passed between them as they decided to try it. They began slowly, very slowly and silently easing forward. Each of them held his pistol by the barrel, ready to knock out the rustlers. Fargo's shoulder was throbbing powerfully now, but he gritted his teeth and concentrated on what the two men were saying.

"Times sure is changed," one said, lighting a cigarette. The other grunted assent. "Ole man Tate's done lost his power, for sure. I can't hardly believe it. Time was we didn't dare set foot on Circle T land. 'Course that was before James and Teddy got all cozied up to the law. And now, I've seen it all. Tonight we waltz in there, pretty as you please, and dance off with Owen Tate's whole goddamn herd. Don't you bet he's fighting mad tonight, the old coot!" In the middle of puffing his cigarette, the rustler started chuckling and then coughed and wheezed.

"I still don't like it," the second one said. "I think Tate's faking it, somehow. He's too smart to get beat. And I don't like this business with the sheriff. All that cozy stuff. I don't trust it. James and his brother are smart, but I think Buck Witchell is gonna double-cross us real soon."

Fargo and Juan were just a few feet behind them now. Fargo wished he could wait to hear what the man had to say about the sheriff, but they couldn't risk the discovery. They raised their pistols high in the air and brought them down heavily on the rustlers' heads at the same time. Juan's was a glancing blow, and the man groaned and struggled as he hit the dirt, but Juan bent immediately and dealt him a second blow that put him out cold.

Fargo bent down and removed his victim's hat, exchanging it for his own. Then he stripped off the man's jacket and put it on, letting the left arm dangle empty. The jacket hid the sling. He took the half-smoked cigarette and held it between his teeth.

119

In the darkness he might pass for the other man. Juan donned the other man's vest and hat. Then they dragged the bodies out of sight. None too soon.

As they were walking back toward the horses, two more men approached.

"Hey, Rusty," one called out. "How's everything?"

Fargo took a puff on the cigarette, keeping his face averted as the glow lit his features.

"Quiet," he muttered, trying to imitate the other man's gruff voice.

"How's it down below?" the other said, coming to stand next to him and look out over the valley. The man puckered his lips and made the owl call. There was a pause. And silence.

Where the hell was Curly, Fargo wondered.

The other man started as the silence continued. "What the hell's going on?"

Then the answer came from just below them.

The man relaxed, then stiffened suddenly. The other one, standing beside Juan, spoke his thoughts in a low voice. "That signal's coming from awfully close. Too damn close. And where are the riders?"

Fargo grabbed his Colt and swung it around, catching the man behind the ear, but it didn't knock him out. Instead, the man feinted back and then, with a yell, lunged forward hitting Fargo square on the left shoulder. Fargo was aware that Juan was struggling with the other rustler too.

Fargo gritted his teeth, trying to club the man with the Colt held in his right hand. He cursed the bullet hole in his shoulder as the man tried to pin him to the ground. Fargo kneed him, and the man jerked back as Fargo delivered a hard blow across his jaw with the pistol butt. As the man's head bounced sideways, Fargo clubbed him, and the man slumped forward. Fargo rolled out from underneath and got to his feet. Juan had knocked out the other one.

His shoulder was screaming in pain now, and Fargo didn't need to feel it to know it was bleeding afresh. The rustler's cry might have been heard by the others higher up the hillside. They had no time to lose.

They continued climbing the slope, which grew rocky. Finally they rounded a stand of sage and stopped. Before them rose a steep cliff, and in the center was the round mouth of a cave. A tattered animal skin hung over the entrance, and golden light leaked out around the edges.

Fargo glanced around—no one else in sight. So far they had dispensed with eight men. He wondered how many more were in the cave with the Spill brothers. Above the cave he saw a wide ledge of rock. Fargo silently pointed to it, and Juan's eyes followed as he indicated a path up one side of the cliff. Juan nodded and made off for it. Fargo edged closer to the cave entrance, grateful for the rustler's hat and jacket. If anyone came out, he would not be recognized as an intruder, at least not at first.

He leaned against the cliff, listening and straining his ears to make out the words being spoken by the voices inside.

"How's she doing?" There was the sound of a movement inside.

"She's out cold. That knock on the head she got will keep her out for a while. She's a slippery one, and if Reyos hadn't been watching out, she'd have gotten away for sure."

Fargo winced in the darkness. So Faith had attempted to escape. And from the sound of things, she had almost succeeded. She had a lot of gumption.

"Bitch," the other said.

"We ought to just let her go. Tate's going to be pissed as hell. It's one thing to steal a man's cattle . . ."

"You're crazy! Tate's an old man. Hell, he can't get the deposit on that land to Deadwood without getting his cowhands killed."

Fargo began to hope that there were only two men in the cave. They had to be James and Theodore—the Spill brothers themselves.

"I wouldn't underestimate Tate," a third voice said.

"That's right, the first voice cut in. "Tate may be old, but he's wily. We should have just left her there."

"Hell, James. Don't you see, this plays right into our hands? Besides, you know about her and Buck Witchell. What do you think old Buck will do when he hears we've got her? He's going to have to up our ante. Hell, I've been telling Buck we're doing all the shit work and he's getting too much of that money. And now that somebody shot his deputy, he's in it all alone. He's going to have to up our take. Here's my plan. Tomorrow we'll send Rusty back to Deadwood with a message to Buck that he can have her if he wants her. Then we'll move that herd farther down south where we'll be safe. Tate will never find us back up in one of those canyons. We'll sit tight till Buck pays up and does whatever he wants with the lady. Then we'll rebrand these cattle and get rid of 'em. In another couple of weeks we're going to be very rich men."

So that was it, Fargo thought. Buck Witchell owed the gang money. But why?

"Screw that money Buck owes us, Ted."

"Hell no. He owes us for every one of those suckers we strung up. That was the deal when he let us escape from jail. And I'm going to get that money too. Every damn dollar of it."

Fargo's thoughts whirled. The men they had strung up? The cowpunchers? Buck Witchell had let them escape from the jail and was paying the rustlers to kill Tate's men?

"And what about those wanted posters?" James asked. "Why did Buck have to go and put those up? I don't like it one bit."

Theodore laughed. "You know the answer to that as well as I do. Buck's gotta keep up appearances. Otherwise he'd never get the signals and find out when the money's coming through."

Fargo didn't have time to wonder what signals they were referring to because just then he heard the whisper of a handful of gravel falling beside him. The sound was too faint to be heard inside, but it told him that Juan was overhead, positioned above the cave entrance. It was time to move. He had heard enough. Now the trick would be to lure the Spill brothers outside before they hurt Faith. He backed away slowly from the cave and ducked behind a large boulder, raised his Colt high above his head, and shot into the air.

The report echoed against the rocks. The animal skin pushed aside, and a man came hurrying out, gun drawn. Fargo waited until he was clear of the cave, then shot him cleanly through the head. The man pitched forward and sprawled in the dust. The light in the cave blinked out. Undoubtedly the Spill brothers had sent the third man out.

He'd have to get them curious—make them think

they had a chance of winning. Then they'd come out and not harm Faith.

"Okay, Ted! You too, James! Come on out. I rode down here alone because I want to talk to you. Man to man," Fargo called.

"Son of a bitch!" he heard James say.

"Who the hell are you?" Theodore Spill called out.

"Who the hell do you think I am?" Fargo shouted back.

There was a long silence.

"Owen . . . Owen Tate?" James answered from inside the cave.

"Damn right," Fargo said. "I've come to get my wife back. I'll pay anything. Even the herd." That would get them curious, he thought. And hopeful. As the skin covering the cave entrance lifted, Fargo wondered himself where the *real* Owen Tate was and why the hell he wasn't here himself.

8

The animal skin at the cave entrance pushed back slowly, revealing the barrel of a rifle. From behind the boulder Fargo could see the blue glint of moonlight on the metal. The blackness of the cave gaped.

"So, where are you, Tate?" It was Theodore Spill's voice.

Fargo held his Colt in his right hand and reached around, grasped the end of the left sleeve which swung loose and held it behind him. His wounded left arm in the sling was hidden by the rustler's jacket he wore. From the front it would look as if he had both arms tied behind his back. He hoped in the darkness he would look and sound like one of the Spill gang. He glanced up and saw Juan crouching over the entrance to the cave. Curly would be coming up any moment, drawn by the pistol shot. Then Fargo stumbled out from behind the rock, as if he were pushed. "He's behind the rock," Fargo said in a gruff voice. "Got me covered." The rustlers fell for it.

"So, what's it going to be, Tate?" Ted Spill called out. "What's the deal?"

Fargo turned his head toward the boulder as if listening to Tate and then looked back toward the cave. "Tate says bring the missus out where he can see her, and he'll throw down his gun. We can have the whole herd in exchange for her. Tate's come alone."

There was a whispered exchange inside the cave and some movement. One of the brothers came easing out of the cave. He held Faith Tate in front of him as cover. She was unconscious and he was struggling to keep her limp body upright.

"Here she is, Tate," Ted's voice said from inside the cave. So, that was James holding Faith, Fargo guessed. "Now, how do we know you'll give us the herd?"

Fargo inclined his head again. "Tate says how does he know we'll let him go?" Fargo measured the distance between him and James Spill holding Faith. He couldn't keep this game going too much longer. He'd slip soon, and the moment they realized he was not one of them, Faith would be dead. Just then James's grip on Faith slipped and she fell to her knees in front of him. In a flash Fargo saw his opportunity.

He dived sideways, simultaneously bringing his Colt around from behind his back. The Colt exploded, the bullet hitting James Spill dead center in the chest. Fargo rolled once and came forward as bullets from the rifle spattered the dust around him. He sprawled on the ground and pumped five bullets one after another into the cave. The bullets richocheted inside with a roar; a man screamed in agony, and then there was silence.

Fargo lay still, his eye on the slumped bodies of James Spill and Faith. James had fallen across her, and she lay unconscious. There was still silence from the cave. Juan waved from above the entrance. Fargo awkwardly reached down and slipped six more bullets from his belt, reloading them slowly. Theodore still might be alive inside the cave, he thought, and armed. He grimly pumped six more bullets into the cave. He heard nothing. Well, he'd have to chance it. He loaded once more and then rose to his feet and stumbled toward Faith. Just as he reached her, out of the corner of his eye, he saw the animal skin move almost imperceptibly. He crouched and fired, again and again. He heard the clatter of a rifle falling on stone. This time he knew he had killed Theodore Spill.

Fargo leaned down and, using his right arm, pulled Faith out from under the dead rustler. She had no wounds. Juan slid down from the hillside just as Curly arrived, panting from his climb up the hillside.

"What happened? Am I too late?" Curly asked. He took off his hat as he saw Faith, assuming she was dead. "Goddamn it," he said.

"She'll come to in a few minutes," Fargo said. "Get her over there." He indicated a spot on the far side of the boulder and away from the mouth of the cave. "I'll go check the cave," he said.

He approached warily, even though he was fairly certain that Theodore Spill had been killed by his last volley. Nothing moved as he reached the animal-skin door and, standing off to the side, jerked it down in a sudden movement.

The faint moonlight spilled into the cave entrance. The notorious rustler lay at the mouth of the cave, his hands clutching nothing, his rifle fallen out of his grasp and lying beside him. His mouth was open in agony, and blood from several bullet wounds darkened the stone. As Fargo's eyes adjusted to the darkness inside the shallow cave, he picked out the shape of a pile of bedrolls on the floor.

Fargo knelt beside Theodore Spill and went

through the contents of his pockets. The man carried a roll of bills, a knife, a tiny derringer, some coins, and a flat disk of polished metal. Fargo put it in his jeans pocket.

The three of them quickly tied the bodies of Theodore and James Spill onto two horses. They bound and gagged the other unconscious rustlers and tied them on horses as well. Then they mounted other horses from the rustlers' remuda. With Curly's help Fargo pulled Faith onto his mount and held her in front of him. Her white stallion was tethered behind. The three of them carefully made their way down the hillside toward the herd.

About half the cattle were on their feet, milling anxiously, stirred by the sound of the gunfire from the hillside. The three riders moved slowly around the huge herd back to where their own horses were tethered.

"I don't think the three of us can control them on a drive north," Curly said doubtfully.

Fargo nodded agreement.

"You and Juan stand guard on them tonight," Fargo said. "When I get to the Circle T, I'll send back some fellows to help you drive them home." He dismounted the rustler's horse and prepared to mount his pinto. Once on the Ovaro, he took Faith up onto the saddle in front of him again, holding her against the crook of his good right arm. "And don't forget to bring the Spill brothers' bodies when you come," Fargo added as he prepared to ride off. "I'll split the reward money with you boys."

Juan and Curly grinned. They remounted their horses and, as Fargo rode over the rise with Faith, he looked back to see the two punchers riding around the herd. One of them whistled the call of the burrowing owl the Spill gang had used. Fargo smiled and answered it before he rode on.

Dawn was a blood red glow on the eastern horizon. The light spilled across the dew-laden chaparral that glittered like diamonds and rubies. His shoulder's throbbing had become so familiar, he hardly noticed it now. He looked down at Faith, her golden hair tangled, her face pale and drawn. She stirred, moving against him. Fargo reined in beside a creek so the pinto and the stallion tethered behind could drink. Faith came to, starting violently as she opened her eyes and realized where she was.

"What . . . what?" Her hand moved instinctively to the back of her head where she had been struck. "Skye . . . the rustlers . . someone shot you . . . you fell. The stampede. I thought you were dead." The tears came to her eyes, and she began sobbing in relief.

"It's all right," he murmured. "We got the Spill brothers, and we got the herd back. Curly and Juan were with me. Everything's going to be all right. We're back on the Circle T, and we'll be home soon." Her sobs continued for a time, and he knew it was the best thing for her. After a few minutes he suggested they get down and have a drink.

They dismounted and took some of the clear, cold water. Fargo splashed it on his face. There was so much he wanted to ask her—so much he wanted to know.

When they had mounted and started off again, slowly so as not to tire the pinto, Fargo told her about the pursuit of the Spill gang, about the cave and the rescue. She shuddered.

"It was horrible," she said. "I pretended to faint, and I tried to get away when they weren't looking."

"And almost made it," Fargo said. "I heard them talking about that. I heard them talk about some other things too. About Buck Witchell, for instance."

Faith stiffened. "The sheriff?" she asked in an odd tone.

"Yeah," Fargo said. "What's this about you and the sheriff?"

He could feel her fear in the way she held her body, suddenly resistant against him. She said nothing as they loped along. He waited, the unanswered question hanging between them.

"Buck Witchell and I . . ." Her voice broke. "It was a long time ago," she said. "After you left St. Louis. I met Buck. I liked him, at first. But he got persistent. Real persistent."

"So you ran," Fargo said.

"That's right," Faith said and then her words came in a torrent. "I tried to leave him so many times, and he wouldn't let me. He would always find me again. He swore he would have me or else. So I fled St. Louis. I came south. First Dallas. He showed up there, too. Then I came on farther, hoping to head out to California. But . . ."

"You got stuck in Deadwood," Fargo said. "And that's when Owen Tate found you."

"Yes. I was safe from Buck Witchell as long as I stayed on the Circle T."

"And then Witchell got himself appointed sheriff," Fargo mused. "Has Buck ever met your husband?"

"Only once," Faith said, her voice faint with remembrance. "The day I left Deadwood, Buck tried to stop me and Owen drew on him. Owen didn't shoot. He just said don't come near me unless you're ready to die. And Buck said he'd get me one way or another. I haven't seen him since."

"The Spill gang was planning to turn you over to Buck Witchell."

"What?" Faith said, wonderingly. "But they're wanted men. There's a reward out for them! Witchell and his posse would shoot them first."

"Apparently not," Fargo said. "The gang's in cahoots with the sheriff." He related the conversation he had heard between the two Spill brothers. She was silent for several minutes.

"That explains a lot," she said.

"It sure does," said Fargo. He thought of the message of the dying boy. It was starting to make sense. Now he knew what the sheriff had to do with the hangings. He was *paying* for them.

It was dangerous information, Fargo thought. And only he had heard the Spill brothers talking about Sheriff Witchell. Now that the rustlers were dead, who would believe his story? If he confronted Buck Witchell, the sheriff would claim he was trying to escape the charge of murdering the deputy.

Fargo thought again about the dying boy's message . . . *The team is against Il Patrone.* And about the Spill brothers. The rustlers were being paid off by the sheriff for hanging the cowpunchers. Undoubtedly they had been splitting the money the punchers were carrying to make the land payment. And somehow the rustlers and the sheriff knew every time the cowpunchers set off to carry a payment to the bank in Deadwood. If the whole team of ranch hands was tipping off the sheriff . . . but the cowpunchers themselves were being hanged. It didn't add up.

Faith passed a weary hand over her face. Fargo saw the strain in her movement. He didn't want to burden her with his suspicions. Not at the moment. Better to talk to Tate himself.

The hacienda was only another mile farther on, and the early morning sun hung bright and low, swiftly drying the dew. The swifts dived through the wide sky, chattering.

The ranch house came into view. A yell rang out from the yard when they were sighted, and Fargo saw several of the men gathering. Others were shouting and running toward the yard.

As they trotted through the gate, Diego hurried forward, worry carved deep in his dark face. "Señora Tate!" he exclaimed. "We were so worried about you!"

"I'm fine," she said, sliding down off the pinto. Fargo heard the note of confidence and strength come into her voice.

"We have trouble, señora," Diego said to her in a low voice.

Several of the ranch hands stepped forward.

"Señora Tate," an older man said, "for almost twenty years I have worked here on the Circle T. My family is here. This is my home."

"Of course it is your home, Matteo," Faith said. She stepped forward and offered him her hand. But he merely looked at it and shook his head.

"I speak for all of us who have been here for a long time, Mrs. Tate," he continued. "Il Patrone has always taken care of us. Has always taken care of the ranch. Now he is not interested in us anymore. He does not come to see us. He asks us to take the money for the new land to the bank. But when our sons are killed for his benefit, he does not come to see them buried." He spat on the ground. "Now the cows are gone. And many of us are dead. Last night four more died. This ranch is cursed and Il Patrone is hiding. He will not show himself. I say he is a coward. I will go away from the Circle T Ranch. I say I will not work for such a man any more."

Matteo turned away. The other men, standing nearby, turned their shoulders as well. Fargo saw them nod their heads. Clearly they all felt the same way. Fargo saw the tears in Faith's eyes, but her jaw tensed.

"Matteo," she said. The force of her voice made him turn back toward her. "Matteo, the herd is not lost. It is safe in Mexico. Curly and Juan are guarding it. You must take some of the men down there to bring the cattle back."

Matteo turned for a moment. "You are a brave señora," Matteo said. "But Il Patrone is hiding behind your skirts. I speak for all of us who live and work on the ranch. Let me talk to Il Patrone himself about the ranch, about many things. Many years ago I came to work for Il Patrone. He made many promises to me. I need to hear these things from his mouth."

Fargo glanced at Faith.

"Come to the hacienda at noon," she said tiredly. "I'm sure that Owen will see you then. I promise he will be there."

Matteo ducked his head. Relief flooded his face. "Gracias, señora," he said. "Others will go now to get the herd back. And I will wait to see Il Patrone."

As they walked toward the hacienda, Fargo reminded her that he also needed to see Owen, to give him the message from the dying cowhand. Faith waved her hand tiredly.

"Yes, yes. I'm sure Owen will see you too. Come to his study at noon. He'll be there then."

Faith looked beaten Fargo noted as she walked tiredly onto the ramada, as if she carried a great weight on her shoulders. He chalked it up to the long night and the knock on her head. But it was something more, he knew. It was about Tate. What could be wrong with the rancher that he didn't want to be seen? The rustlers had said he was an old man. Was that it? The fear of being seen old and weak?

Faith climbed the stairs slowly with scarcely a backward glance. Fargo went to his room and lay down on the bed, fully clothed. He was too tired to take care of his shoulder. In moments sleep won out over the dull throbbing.

Inez woke him well before noon, bringing in a tray of oatcakes and coffee. Fargo rose and stripped off the rustler's jacket he was still wearing. Inez cried out when she saw the blood-stained sling, her round face aghast.

"Dio! Señor Fargo! You did not even say you were shot! Stay right here, and I will return with medicines!"

"Gracias," Fargo said. As soon as she left, he pulled the tray toward him and quickly polished off most of the breakfast. He was hungry and needed strength. And he knew he would not feel like eating after they finished cleaning the bullet wound.

When she returned, he was washing his face. She carried a large pot of warm water, towels, and ointments. Fargo could see she had cared for bullet wounds before.

Fargo took a seat at the table and Inez began to tug slowly at the sling. Her fat fingers were deceptively delicate. The blood and silt from the stream had dried the fabric of the sling to the wound, and she had to wet it down to get it loose. Even with her care, the wound began to bleed again. It hurt, but not all that much.

In a half hour she had cleaned out the wound, applied ointments and a fresh bandage, and had tied a new sling around his neck. The throbbing was replaced now by a sharp pain from the salve, but Fargo knew it would subside and then there would be weeks of stiffness. Maybe months. Still, for a gunshot wound, it wasn't the worst he'd ever had.

"Bueno," Fargo said, smiling and moving his left arm in the sling to show her that it felt better. "Mucho gracias."

Inez smiled broadly and ducked her head. "Very brave man," she said, packing away the medical supplies.

"Where is Faith . . . Mrs. Tate?" Fargo asked.

Her dark eyes grew opaque. "She is upstairs," Inez answered. "But at noon, Mr. Tate will be in his study to talk to Matteo. Then he will see you."

Fargo followed her out and took a seat in the large room down the hall from Owen's study. All was quiet. A few minutes later Matteo appeared at the front door and was ushered inside. He took a seat opposite Fargo and smiled nervously. The old man had removed his felt hat and was twisting it in his hands.

At the sound of footsteps the door to Owen Tate's study opened. Diego came out and crossed the room, gesturing for Matteo to follow. The door shut, and Fargo listened to the muffled sound of voices for five minutes or so. The door opened again, and Matteo exited, closing the door behind him.

He crossed the room to Fargo. "He looks very weak, Il Patrone," Matteo said, worry showing in his face. "He is . . . changed. Even his voice is weak. But what he said is still the same. I will tell the others. We must stay for the sake of the ranch. Il Patrone has told me again that it is my home. And him I believe."

Matteo left, and in another moment Diego came out and gestured for Fargo to follow. The study was dark, heavy curtains masking the wide windows. Fargo peered through the darkness toward the high desk chair that was turned away from him. Diego closed the door and stood quietly. His voice broke the long silence.

"Señor Tate. Mr. Fargo is here."

The chair slowly turned around, and Fargo was shocked to see a small, thin man in baggy clothes, his features hardly visible below the leather hat he was unaccountably wearing indoors. A fluffy white beard hid his jawline and billowed down the front of his leather jacket. He extended one hand and laid it on the desk in front of him. He was wearing leather gloves.

"My wife says you have an important message for me." The voice was soft, scarcely above a whisper. Fargo, shocked by Owen Tate's appearance, took a moment to find his voice. In the silence he tried to picture Faith Lawrence married to the man in front of him. But it was almost impossible.

Fargo glanced at Diego, standing beside the door. He did not want to give the message to Owen Tate within hearing of anyone else. Tate's eyes glittered in the darkness beneath the deep brim of his hat. He crooked one gloved finger and Diego nodded, stepped out, and closed the door behind him.

"I was riding east of Deadwood and came across four of your cowpokes. They had just been hanged," Fargo started. There was something odd about Owen Tate, his mind was telling him. As he spoke, he tried to place what it was. "One of them was still alive. Just," he continued. "I found out later his name was Pablo. He gave me this message and made me promise to deliver it only to Il Patrone and to no one else." Fargo paused, hoping Owen Tate would speak again in that intriguing whisper. But no sound came. After a full minute of silence, Tate nodded his head slowly. Fargo continued.

"He said this." Fargo paused as he summoned the memory of the boy's exact words and phrasing to his mind. "Team works for the sheriff. Team is against Il Patrone now." Yes, he was sure he had said it just as the boy had. Fargo watched Owen Tate carefully, but there wasn't a flicker of movement. They waited another long moment, each regarding the other. Then Tate nodded very slowly.

"Thank you," he whispered. "For . . . everything. You will be rewarded." Without waiting for anything further from Fargo, Tate picked up a heavy iron paperweight and rapped on the table. The door opened immediately, and Diego came in to usher Fargo out of the room.

Hell, Fargo thought as he walked down the hallway—that was hardly the image he had of the powerful rancher everyone feared. Still there was something compelling about the man . . . the way he handled himself. And something strange that tugged on him like an old memory. Fargo shook off the feeling and spotted Inez coming out of the kitchen.

"Where is Faith?" he asked. She smiled at him familiarly.

"She is upstairs, but will be down soon." Her dark eyes darted to the study door.

"Yes, I just saw Mr. Tate," Fargo said. "Is he ill?"

Inez nodded slowly. "He is a very old man," she said in a toneless voice and turned back toward the kitchen.

Fargo stepped outside to check on the Ovaro in the stable. When he returned to the hacienda, Faith was coming outside onto the ramada. Her face was pink and moist, and he imagined she had just scrubbed it as he caught a whiff of soap. But her eyes were troubled. They sat down side by side.

"Owen told me about the message," she said. "I don't know what to make of it."

"What does Owen think?" Fargo asked.

There was a slight hesitation in her voice. "He didn't say."

With a silence between them Fargo was sure that Faith knew what he was thinking. Owen Tate was a very old and probably dying man, and Fargo still had a lot of questions he wanted answered.

But before Fargo could ask them, she continued. "If the whole team of ranch hands is against Il Patrone, then we haven't got a chance of anything," she said. "And we've only got enough money for one more payment on the land. If this gets stolen, we won't have enough to try again until next spring. And if we lose that central tract of land, the Circle T ranch is done for."

Fargo nodded. He looked out across the yard and beyond the thick adobe wall to the wide rolling ranch spreading to the horizon. Then he spotted a plume of dust. A man riding fast, coming from the north. Fargo narrowed his eyes and recognized the form of Hank. They stood as he galloped through the gate and into the yard. He dismounted and hurried up to the ramada, shooting a dirty look at Fargo.

"One of the line riders got a message that there was a telegram came in for you in Deadwood." Hank drew a piece of paper from his shirt pocket and handed it across to Faith. "It's bad news," he added, his voice sharp.

Faith unfolded the paper and read it. Then she handed it wordlessly to Fargo.

RECEIVED OTHER OFFER FOR LAND STOP PAYMENT MUST BE DEPOSITED IN DEADWOOD BANK BY SUNDOWN OR WILL SELL TO OTHER BUYER STOP FERNANDO DE ESTRELLA

"I must go right now," she said, a hardness in her voice. "I will go myself, if I have to crawl on my knees, goddamn it. That money will get to the bank or I will die trying."

Fargo laid a hand on her arm. "Don't, Faith," he said. "I'll take the payment for you."

"No," she said. "I'm going too. It's my ranch. I must." Fargo saw that she would not be dissuaded. Hank stood watching them, looking from one to the other.

"I'd like to come and help," he said. Faith smiled at him. "We'll get through, Miz Tate, or my name's not Tim Hankins!"

"That's brave of you Hank," she said. "Thank you. We'll have to ride out immediately to make it to Deadwood before sundown."

"I'll get the horses ready," Hank said. He puffed his chest out and strutted off across the yard, his spindly legs bowed outward. Fargo saw Matteo hurrying across the yard. He spotted them and came over.

"Gracias, Señora, for the opportunity to speak with Il Patrone," Matteo said. "He said so many wise things. It was just like the old days, even though he has become very weak. But it made my heart strong just to see him and talk with him again."

"I'm sure," Faith said, sounding distracted. "Listen, Matteo. Fargo and Hank and I are going to deliver that payment to Deadwood. Right now."

Matteo's jaw went slack even as Fargo wondered if Faith was being prudent by letting anyone else know what they were up to.

"No, señora, please. You should not do this dangerous thing. You know what has happened to every one of the ranch hands who has carried the money to Deadwood." He made a gesture across his throat.

"The Spill brothers are dead now," Faith said. "So that will not happen to us. This time we will get to Deadwood. And by tonight, all will be well."

Matteo shook his head sadly, the fear still darkening his eyes. "The men will be back with the herd very soon," he said. "Please wait for them. Then many, many men can all go together. All the men of the Circle T will ride with you. I will tell them about my talk with Il Patrone, and they will have courage again, just like in the old days. They will come with you, and then you will be safe."

Fargo glanced up at the afternoon sun. It was several hours' ride back to Deadwood. Hank had saddled their three horses and waited in the yard.

"I can't wait for them, Matteo," she said. "We don't have much time." Faith hurried into the house.

"Please take care of her, señor," Matteo said softly. "She is Mr. Tate's heart. Without her Il Patrone would die. And without him the ranch will perish."

Fargo nodded. She reappeared with a leather pouch, undoubtedly the payment, which she stowed in an inside pocket of her white leather jacket.

Just as they were mounting, Juan walked into the yard. He hurriedly saddled his horse and joined them. They rode out immediately, Hank in the lead, Faith second with Juan, and Fargo bringing up the rear.

The wide open land was devoid of punchers and cattle as they rode along. The ranch hands who weren't herding the cattle back from Mexico were left at the line camps, although clearly the Spill gang had been able to slip by them and onto the ranch.

The four of them galloped hard for several hours, flying over the gently folded grassland, avoiding the prairie-dog holes.

Then the patches of mesquite and sage sprouted on the plain, and they began to descend toward the Nueces River. Finally they came to the last ridge, overlooking the oak-shaded riverbed and sage-thicketed land on the opposite bank.

Fargo's keen eyes swept the scene, but he could see nothing moving in all the landscape. He tried to pick out the Buckhorn Trail, but the track was lost in the chaparral. Then he glanced at Hank who was looking down at his horse's hooves.

"Trouble?" Fargo asked.

Hank dismounted. "Got a little problem with the shoe," he muttered. "You ride on and cross the river. I'll catch up with you in just a minute." Fargo nodded and set off right away, plunging down the bank. Faith and Juan were hard pressed to keep up.

"Come on," he said as they approached the stand of live oak down by the river. As soon as they reached the cover of the trees, he reined in and dismounted. "Get down," he said to them. When Faith and Juan were on the ground, he pulled them to the edge of the trees, back toward the slope they had just descended. They were just in time to catch sight of Hank sitting astride his horse. He was holding something high in the air and gazing across the river.

"What's he doing?" Faith asked, fear in her voice.

Fargo reached into the pocket of his jeans and drew forth the polished metal disk he had taken from Theodore Spill's body and showed it to them.

"He's signaling Buck Witchell," Fargo said. "I wondered how the sheriff and the Spill gang got word of the payments heading to Deadwood. They used mirrors and the reflecting sun. I saw one of these hanging off the sheriff's saddle. I wondered what the hell it was."

"But . . . Hank?" Faith said, her voice quavering in disbelief. "Tim Hankins a traitor? I can't believe it."

"Who would believe it of Tim?" Juan said wonderingly, too surprised as yet to feel anger.

Fargo suddenly started. "What did you say?" he asked Juan.

"I said who would believe it—" Juan repeated.

"Of Tim," Fargo cut in, mimicking Juan's accent. He pronounced the name "team." "Tim is against Il Patrone!" he said excitedly. "That's what Pablo was trying to tell me . . ."

"Of course!" Faith said. "It was Tim Hankins all along. Not the others!" Juan looked from one to the other, confused by their conversation but beginning to comprehend that Hankins was responsible for the murder of the cowhands.

"Keep ahold on yourself," Fargo said to Juan whose face had begun to flush dark, his black eyes flashing with rage. "We'll get our revenge soon enough."

Fargo's eyes swept the hillside again, seeking and finding the distant figure of Tim Hankins sitting on his horse at the top of the rise. He was making no move to follow them but was looking across the river.

"I bet the sheriff will be here any moment," Fargo said. The three of them hurried back to their horses and mounted. "This way." Fargo gestured, intending to lead them along the bank of the river under the cover of the oaks and out of sight of Tim Hankins sitting high on the hill. They could get a good quarter mile away and then cut across the river before Hankins realized which way they'd gone.

But there was a sudden flurry of movement as Juan drew his rifle from his saddle sheath and, with a sputtered Spanish curse, he spurred his horse in the direction of Tim Hankins.

"Juan! No!" Faith called. Fargo started out after the cowpuncher, hoping to stop him before he galloped out into the open, but he had too much of a head start. Juan dashed out from under the trees, his rifle raised and pointed toward Hank. He fired, and Fargo heard the resounding crack of a rifle from above. He reined in the Ovaro as he saw Juan slump forward onto the neck of his horse. It was too late. Hank had been ready. And now Hank knew that they'd figured him out. In another moment Hank would be coming down the hill after them. Fargo drew his Sharps rifle.

Just then, Fargo caught the sound of hoofbeats from across the river. Goddamn it, he thought in a flash. The posse had been across the river all along, hiding in the sage thickets and waiting for this ambush.

"Ride!" he shouted to Faith as he spurred the Ovaro.

9

A bullet thwacked through the leaves overhead, followed by a second that ricocheted off a rock nearby and kicked up a fan of dust. Hank was firing into the stand of oak and hoping for a lucky hit. Faith spurred her stallion, and Fargo followed as they galloped along the riverbank. Hell, he thought, with Hank on one side of them and the posse across the river, they were trapped.

Fargo glanced back and across the water, expecting to see two dozen men on horseback crashing out of the chaparral on the opposite bank. His hopes rose when he saw only Buck Witchell, his horse halfway across in pursuit. Even from this distance Fargo could discern Buck's tall muscular frame and the bright blond hair around his darkly tanned face. So Buck Witchell had received the message from Hank. But where was the rest of the posse?

Buck sighted them and raised his rifle slowly. Fargo raised his, and they exchanged fire. A bullet zinged by his head, and he saw the sheriff recoil and clutch his leg. Fargo urged the Ovaro faster.

Another flurry of fire erupted around them—four, five, six shots. Hank was close enough to use his pistol and was shooting blind. Fargo holstered the rifle. Ahead of him Faith's stallion stumbled, and Fargo saw that it had been hit in the flank. The white horse screamed, reared up, and faltered. Faith, white-faced and grim, clung to the horse's back, clutching the reins.

Fargo brought the Ovaro close. The pinto, smelling the other horse's blood, whinnied but obeyed. Most horses would have panicked, he thought, as he dropped the reins with his good right arm and reached out toward Faith. The stallion's front legs had come down to earth, and it took a faltering step as it began to fall. He seized her arm and pulled her toward him, just as the stallion sank to its knees, shuddering.

Faith struggled onto the saddle in front of him as Fargo drew his pistol and shot the doomed horse in the head. He glanced back. The sheriff was climbing up the bank of the river. Fargo could hear the hoofbeats of Hank's mount charging down the hill, although he was still hidden by the oak trees.

The Ovaro leaped forward. Fargo bent over, his good arm holding the reins, Faith hunkered down in front of him, flinging herself across the neck of the pinto. Fargo concentrated on their speed, giving the pinto a loose rein, but keeping his eyes on the rough terrain ahead. He gave the animal subtle direction with his knees as they pounded up onto the rough sage plain.

The horse seemed to fly along the ground, its muscular legs hammering the dirt, its long lean sides expanding and contracting as it breathed with the effort. Shots split the air around them, but as the minutes passed, Fargo realized they were almost out of firing range.

The Ovaro was foaming and sweating under the weight of two people. There weren't many horses could do that. Fargo patted the side of the pinto's neck but kept his knees tight, not letting the horse ease up on speed. He glanced about at the terrain across the river, looking for familiar landmarks. They'd have to ford the Nueces soon, he realized. He reckoned they were a couple of miles from Deadwood. When they reached the town, they'd be only a few minutes ahead of Hank and the sheriff. This would be a close one.

"You all right?" he asked Faith, as he straightened up.

"Just scared," she said. He didn't waste his breath with any more talk and neither did she. They needed all their concentration.

Finally Fargo glanced back. Far in the distance, against the white-hot horizon, he saw a blur of dust. Hank and the sheriff were a couple of miles behind them already. Time to cross the river.

The Ovaro forded quickly, emerging dripping wet on the opposite bank. They didn't have time to pause and let it drink. The pinto seemed to understand intuitively, forging up the riverbank and springing ahead into a fast gallop as it climbed the rise toward the Buckhorn Trail. They gained the track in moments, swinging onto it and heading west into Deadwood.

The sun hung low on the horizon. There wasn't much time, Fargo thought. Any delay now, and the bank might close before they arrived. They were galloping hell-bent, making good time on the wide, dusty track bordered by dense thickets of sage. Deadwood lay just ahead.

They galloped around a curve of the trail and the horse neighed. Riding toward them, spread out across the trail, was the sheriff's posse. More than twenty men. All armed.

Fargo tensed. They'd have to try to bust through,

he thought, urging the Ovaro forward. But the men ahead of him reacted quickly and drew their rifles in an instant. Faith gasped and shrank against him. If any of them fired, she would get hit first, Fargo realized. He reined in.

The posse surrounded them. Fargo pulled his hat down low, hoping no one would recognize him.

"Why it's Faith Lawrence . . . I mean, Mrs. Tate," one of them said in a shocked voice. "You've been riding fast."

The pinto was foaming with sweat and pawed the ground anxiously. The stringy horses of the posse shifted under the men.

"We haven't seen you around Deadwood since you got married, Miz Tate," another said. Most of the men holstered their guns. Fargo couldn't quite read the man's tone. It wasn't anger. Nor was it threatening. It was . . . curiosity? Fargo began to wonder if the men in the posse knew that Buck Witchell had been in league with the Spill brothers. There was no time to find out.

"We can't talk now," Faith said, her voice tight with tension. "We're in a hurry. Come, ride with us into Deadwood."

"Why are you going to Deadwood?" one of them asked in a tone that said he had all the time in the world.

"Hey!" said a skinny man in a black shirt. He was leaning over, trying to peer at Fargo's lowered face. "I know you!"

Fargo's hopes sank. He'd been recognized.

Several of the other men drew their pistols.

"You're the man we ran into on the trail with Lucia," the skinny man said. "You're the one who shot the deputy and ran."

The men muttered darkly, and more drew their pistols. Fargo felt Faith stiffen with fear.

"Sheriff Buck says you're the one who's been helping out the Spill brothers," the black shirt continued.

Fargo realized he had about one minute to talk them out of this. The sheriff and Hank would be riding up any moment. And that could only make matters worse.

"That's ridiculous," Fargo said, looking around at the men. "I shot and killed both Spill brothers last night." Fargo waited for their reaction, which would tell him if the men in the posse were in on Buck Witchell's little game or not.

There was a shocked silence.

"You shot the Spill brothers?" one man muttered. There was awe in his voice. "Is that true?"

"It sure is," Faith answered hotly.

"Hell . . ." the skinny one said, eyeing Fargo. "That's a lot better than we've been doing. We've been chasing them forever. Every time the sheriff led us one place, we'd find out later that the Spill gang was some place else."

Fargo realized the time had come to put all the cards on the table. And he was pretty sure it was a good bet. "That's because Buck Witchell has been working with the Spill brothers," he said.

"What?" The men mumbled and muttered in confusion. Just then, Fargo heard hoofbeats. He glanced back. The sheriff and Hank would ride into view any instant. It was now or never.

"Follow me!" he shouted, urging the pinto forward. The men, still confused and wondering, let him pass through at a gallop; then they spurred their mounts and followed him down the trail.

The tilted sign for the town of Deadwood flashed

by them. Fargo wondered wryly how many more population figures would be crossed out before the day was over. The dusty street was deserted. Straight ahead of them, far beyond the tired town of Deadwood, the now-golden sun was touching the horizon. Fargo reined in before the big mud-brick bank building. He and Faith dismounted and approached the door. A small dapper man was just hanging the closed sign in the front window. He looked through the pane and shook his head. Fargo shoved open the door.

"We're just closing," the little man said, anxiously smoothing his baldness. He glanced through the doorway at the posse dismounting in the street.

"The lady has a deposit to make," Fargo said. The little man shook his head firmly and opened his mouth to speak again.

"Oh, please. Please," Faith cut in. The banker glanced at her and then softened.

"Sure," he said, smoothing his head again. "Come in, ma'am." He stepped backward and ushered them in. "Anything for a lady. We don't get many ladies coming through Deadwood . . ." Fargo realized the man was going to start chattering. They had to hurry. If the sheriff arrived before the deposit was in, there was no telling what would happen.

"Come right this way," the banker said. He pulled the green eyeshade onto his head and let himself into the teller's cage. Faith pulled the bulging leather packet out of her jacket and shoved it under the bars. Several of the men from the posse pushed inside the doorway behind them and the others crowded outside, looking in through the window. The banker opened the leather wallet and took out the stack of bills. Then he glanced up at Faith, who was looking anxiously toward the door.

"I've only been in Deadwood for a year," the banker said, peeling off the bills and counting them slowly. "I don't think I've ever seen you around here before," he said with a flirtatious smile, glancing up at her. He lost count and had to start over. Faith bit her lip.

Fargo slid around beside Faith and suddenly drew his Colt, pointing it directly at the teller.

Several of the men in the posse gasped. The teller looked up in alarm to see the pistol aimed straight at him. "Is . . . is this a holdup?" he asked. Behind him Fargo heard some of the posse drawing their weapons.

"No," Fargo said. "This is a deposit. The gun is to help you concentrate. I want you to give the lady the deposit receipt in one minute—made out to Mrs. Owen Tate. One minute, starting now." Fargo began counting slowly.

Several of the men from the posse sniggered and holstered their pistols. Others, not knowing what to make of it, kept their guns trained on Fargo.

The bank teller fell to counting the money with furious speed. Drops of sweat dotted his bald pate. He hastily wrote out a receipt and slipped it under the bars by the time Fargo counted to fifty.

"Well done," Fargo said, holstering his Colt. Several of the men standing at the doorway laughed in relief. Fargo heard hoofbeats outside and a shout. The crowd of men stirred as Buck Witchell came shoving his way inside. Blood soaked one thigh where Fargo had shot him as he rode across the Nueces River.

"Where's that money?" Buck yelled, his face dark with fury, his pistol drawn and wavering before him. He had lost his hat and his bright blond hair shone even in the dimness of the bank's interior. His sun-bleached eyebrows were lowered over eyes that seemed to have lost their focus. "You!" he said, sighting Fargo. "Goddamn you. Hand over that money you're . . . you're trying to steal."

"I'm trying to steal?" Fargo said with a laugh that barked disbelief. "I have just accompanied Mrs. Tate to make a deposit. That money, which rightfully belongs to Owen Tate, is now safely in the bank."

"Give me that money," the sheriff shouted, looking about wildly. He sighted the teller in his cage and advanced on him, his pistol shaking with fury.

"The . . . the . . . lady has just made a deposit," the teller said, wincing with fear. "That's legal like. I can't give you the money unless a judge tells me to. That's the law, sheriff."

"I'm the goddamn law in this town!" Buck Witchell shouted, enraged. The men at the door drew back in fear, whispering to each other. "And if I say give me that money, you will! I'll be goddamned if I'm going to let Owen Tate buy that blasted land after he stole my woman!" The sheriff was lurching back and forth now, waving his pistol, clearly out of his mind. His darting eyes suddenly locked onto Faith, huddled against the teller's cage.

"Come on, Faith," Buck Witchell said, his voice cracking. He stumbled across the floor. The leg was bleeding bad, Fargo saw. The blood from it made a bright red pool across the wooden planks. "You know you love me. You always have. I know you do." His voice was crazed, pleading with her. Faith shook her head wildly, shrinking against the wall. Fargo moved his hand very slowly toward his Colt. Very slowly.

"Faith," Witchell said again, his voice a ravaged whisper, "I've got you. I've saved up money, see. The money I took from your boys. I can buy your land. Tate's an old man. He can't give you what you want. I can. You know I can. And Tate's almost finished. The ranch is almost done for. Don't you see? I'm going to set you free."

Buck Witchell lurched toward Faith, one hand reaching out for her as Fargo drew and fired. The first bullet tore the sheriff's pistol from his grasp. It clattered across the floor. Then Fargo fired a second time, catching Witchell in the temple. Buck fell, hand outstretched, and clutched at the hem of Faith's skirt with his last strength as he died.

Faith screamed and pulled away, her knees suddenly weak. Fargo was beside her quickly to catch her as she collapsed against him. There was a somber silence in the room.

"Son of a bitch," one of the posse said quietly. Faith sobbed silently in Fargo's one-armed embrace.

There was another stir at the door, and several of the men in the posse pushed Tim Hankins forward. One of the men removed the gun from Hank's holster, and he didn't protest, but stood with his head lowered. Faith looked up.

"Tim!" she said. "How could you do this? To me . . . to Mr. Tate? To the rest of the boys?"

Hankins remained staring at the floor.

"I got friendly with Buck," Hank said. Fargo thought of the handcuffs. Of course, Hankins had got them from his friend Witchell. "Buck told me . . . he told me that Mr. Tate wasn't really such a good man. And he promised me that if I signaled him when the payment deliveries were planned, he'd give me some of the money. And that . . . that I would have my own ranch someday."

"But, Tim, the Circle T belongs to you. It belongs to all of us," Faith said.

"You know what I mean," he said, glancing up at her. "My own ranch. Like Tate has his own ranch."

"That's not the way to get it," Fargo cut in. Hankins hung his head again.

"Let's lock him up," one of the posse said. They bustled him out the door. The skinny man with the black shirt approached Faith.

"Miz Tate?" he said, ducking his head in embarrassment. "I got a confession to make. Now that we heard all that Buck Witchell had to say, I think I am beginning to understand some things. I seem to remember a time around here when us folks in Deadwood didn't hold nothing against Mr. Tate. He was just a neighbor like anybody else. But now I realize that starting when Buck Witchell got here, we gradually began to think of Mr. Tate as some kind of villain. I think Buck Witchell changed our minds so slowly that none of us knew what was happening. And that ugliness just infected the whole town. Now I understand why." He flushed, turning bright red from the neck up. "I'd just like to say, ma'am, that you'd always be welcome again in Deadwood. And Mr. Tate too."

Faith shook his hand and then shook hands with the other men standing around. Fargo followed her outside. She mounted Hank's horse, and Fargo took his seat on the Ovaro. They trotted slowly out of Deadwood, watching the shadows lengthen on the chaparral.

The first stars had come out when they halted by the Nueces. They had scarcely spoken. They watched the horses drink.

"Let's go tell Owen that the ranch is safe," Faith

said, sadness in her voice. Fargo agreed, and they rode on as the darkness of night gathered.

A mile from the hacienda Faith suddenly galloped ahead, angling toward a stream some distance from the ranch house. He followed. They came to a grove of live oak, and she dismounted, leading the horse to a small hillock. Fargo got off the pinto and followed.

He came upon her, resting one hand against the trunk of a tree and looking down at the ground. "I thought we were going to talk to Owen," he said, wondering why she had changed her mind.

"We are," she said. He followed her gaze and, in the darkness, made out the subtle shape of an unmarked grave on the ground.

"Owen fell ill last year. He died two months ago," Faith said. Fargo's thoughts reeled. "Just after the first punchers were hanged."

"That . . . that was you in the study," Fargo said, "pretending to be Owen." He thought of the frail and mysterious figure in the hat and gloves and long white beard. "And the morning I came in and found his chair warm?"

"That was me too," Faith said. "I had been working on the accounts."

"Yes," she went on tiredly. "I started impersonating Owen even before he died. When he was too sick to meet with his men, Owen had the idea. He didn't want anyone to know how bad his illness was. It was easy. I had listened to him run the ranch for so long that I knew just what he would say. Only Inez and Diego knew the secret. Owen insisted that they were the only ones I could really trust."

"And after the trouble started . . ." Fargo said.

"From the first hangings, Owen and I knew that

somebody on the ranch was in on it. So we were even more afraid the traitor would know he was weak and take advantage of it," Faith said. "Everybody always said that without Owen Tate, the Circle T would collapse. But now . . ."

"Now you have the deeds to all the land," Fargo said. "The ranch is safe." He paused for a moment. "But, Faith . . ." The next words were almost too painful to speak.

She said them for him. "Why didn't I tell you?" she said. He glanced across at her and even in the darkness under the trees, he could see the tears on her cheeks. "I guess I got in the habit of keeping the secret," she said. "I knew I could trust you, but . . . but I was still afraid."

Fargo looked out beyond the trees to the dark plain. "And what now?" he asked.

He felt her warm hand against the bark of the tree, searching for his. He grasped it.

"Tonight my husband will die in his sleep," Faith said. "Tomorrow we'll bury him. Inez and Diego will fill the coffin with stones. Now that the Circle T is safe, Owen Tate can finally rest in peace."

They stood for a while listening to the night sounds. A coyote yowled miles and miles away.

"And then?" He gave her hand a squeeze.

"You'll stay on the ranch for a while." He heard the smile in her voice. "Until your shoulder heals. And then you'll move on. And someday you'll ride through again."

Fargo nodded into the darkness. It had always been like this between him and Faith. She let go of his hand. They mounted and rode silently to the hacienda.

LOOKING FORWARD!

**The following is the opening
section from the next novel in the exciting
Trailsman series from Signet:**

THE TRAILSMAN #137
MOON LAKE MASSACRE

*1860, Utah—land of saints
and sinners where some tried to build
the future on greed and killing . . .*

They were still shadowing him. The big man astride
the magnificent Ovaro let his lake blue eyes squint
into the setting sun. The six riders had been trailing
him most of the day, staying well back in the bur
oak and shadbush. But he had spotted the slender
shape of bows slung across the shoulders of two of
the riders, and he'd caught the glint of sun on red-
brown torsos. This was the Utah Territory, mostly
Ute country though sometimes the Arapaho ventured into it. It was a land that in some places was
rich and green and in others dry and parched. Hap-
pily he rode through the rich, green terrain of low
hills well-covered with good shade trees.

The six riders bothered him but not simply because they'd been trailing him. It was how they
were doing it that nagged at him. It wasn't normal
for six braves to trail their quarry most of the day.

There had been plenty of places they could have come at him, numerous spots where he'd been ready and waiting, expecting an attack. But none had come. They had continued to hang back, seemingly content to just trail him. It was almost as if they waited to see where he was going. Very strange indeed, he frowned to himself as the sun began to drop over the distant hills. The blackness of night would quickly descend, he knew, and he found a spot to bed down under the tapering leaves of a bur oak.

Skye Fargo decided to leave the saddle on the horse, just in case, and as night enveloped the land he made a small fire. He set his bedroll beside the fire and stretched out to heat some beef strips from his saddlebag. They were still in the trees, watching. They hadn't gone their way. He felt it, knew it. But they were too far away to see much but the shape of him in the glow of the small fire. He slowly chewed the dried beef strips and again wondered why six braves had wasted a day shadowing him. Was it merely a harbinger of stranger things to come? The letter in his pocket had certainly hinted at devious turns. Perhaps the actions of the six Indians was simply a reflection of the spirit of this Utah territory, a land where those who professed themselves saints and those who plainly were sinners staked their respective claims. In this land perhaps God and the devil were both bystanders.

Yet he had come, drawn by old memories and old loyalties, and he took the letter from his pocket and read it again by the fire's light.

Dear Skye Fargo,

I am writing on account of an old friend of yours, Ben Adams. He needs help but he is too stubborn and too proud to ask for it. He has often talked about you and so I am writing this to you. He'd be real mad at me if he knew.

As Ben's friend, I know he is afraid and into more than he can handle and I am afraid for him. I don't want to put him in any more danger than he is now so I won't meet you here at Moon Lake. But there's a village named Duchess nearby in the north Utah Territory.

I'll go there on July 6th and stay at the Inn for three days. I hope you can meet me there for Ben's sake. He's told me you ride a fine Ovaro so I'll know you when you arrive.

After you cross the White River and go over the hills, find an old ox trail. Take it north and it'll lead you right into Duchess. Thank you.

Ellie Willis

Fargo folded the letter back into his pocket. Ben Adams had been a good friend of his father's, a dear friend who stood by his pa when the times were hardest. Fargo always wanted to find a way to repay Ben Adams, but in time the man had moved away and the debt was still unpaid. Maybe this was the chance, at last. Ben had written him a few times over the years, reaching him care of General Delivery at the Springfield Post Depot, just where this letter had finally reached him.

He had taken off at once, realizing July sixth wasn't that far away. But he'd made good time, and he expected he'd be reaching Duchess by tomorrow, only a day late. The letter had evoked old memories, but it had raised more questions than answers, and he looked forward to meeting Ellie Willis. He let the small fire go out and sat in the inky blackness for a moment, then slid from the bedroll. He took a blanket, wrapped it around himself and sank into the nearby brush. The Colt in his hand, he let himself sleep, certain he'd hear any attack on the bedroll.

But the night passed quietly and he woke with the dawn sun, used his canteen to wash, and breakfasted on a stand of wild blackberry. He surveyed the land as he rolled up his bedroll and only the flash of a Bullock's oriole broke the calm with a brief explosion of orange and black. He unsaddled the Ovaro and used a body brush from his knapsack to go over the horse's coat with a quick grooming. When he saddled up again, he headed the horse downward through the hills, the sun glistening on the jet black fore- and hindquarters and pure white midsection. He rode slowly, making no direct glances but letting himself scan the tree cover to his rear, and finally he spotted the silent forms again trailing him and again staying back.

He frowned as he rode. What were they waiting for, he asked himself again. It was not usual Indian behavior simply to follow, and he purposely made his way through a narrow passage, the Colt in his hand, waiting for them to attack. But no attack came in the perfect place for one, and he emerged and rode up the side of the next low hill. The white river was long behind him, and he saw the last of the hills loom up ahead as he rode on with the sun moving into midafternoon. The silent riders still followed, still stayed in the trees when he moved down out of the last of the low hills.

Three trails furrowed the land, one far too narrow, the second one heading over a series of rocky mounds no ox-drawn wagons would have taken, and the third plainly the old ox trail, wide enough for wagons and flat enough for oxen. He paused for a long moment as he surveyed the three trails and then turned the pinto down the ox trail. His glance went to both sides of the trail where thick growths of box elder rode up, and he cast a glance behind him as he rode. The gray-purple haze of dusk had begun to filter down when he spotted the movement in the trees, no longer to his rear but in the foliage alongside the road. Their stalking and trailing was over, Fargo knew, and he drew the Colt at the same time as he dug his heels into the Ovaro's ribs.

The horse leaped forward and went into an instant gallop and Fargo half turned in the saddle, the Colt upraised, waiting for the Indians to come out of the trees and onto the road. He was confident of picking off at least two as they came into the open but, as he frowned in surprise, they stayed in the tree cover, and he saw the arrows hurl toward him. They were wild, and Fargo kept the horse running forward, casting frowning glances into the trees as the Indians continued to remain there and the dusk grew deeper. He didn't understand any of it. They couldn't ride fast enough to keep up with him if they stayed in the trees, and yet they did, and he saw another cluster of arrows fly his way, again off the mark.

But suddenly he heard the sound of rifle fire and he turned, ducked low as two shots came close. Staying low in the saddle, he swerved the horse as another pair of shots resounded. As he steered the Ovaro toward the trees at his right, he saw another four arrows hurtle through the air toward him. He raced into the trees, yanked the horse to a stop, and aimed the Colt at the three horsemen charging toward him. His first two shots missed as his targets were mostly hidden in the foliage, but he heard the grunt of pain as his third shot connected. He waited, Colt ready to fire, but the three riders turned, half hidden in the trees as they raced away.

Fargo heard the hooves at his left and saw the three near-naked riders crossing the road toward him, one with a rifle he fired into the trees, spraying shots in a wide pattern. Fargo dropped from the saddle as the bullets slammed into the branches at his back. He returned fire from on one knee, and again the attackers peeled away and ran. The first three were already out of sight in the gray dimness of dusk, and Fargo leaped onto the Ovaro and sent the horse racing down to the road where the other three Indians were fleeing. They were starting to turn to race back into the trees when he took aim, fired, and saw one topple from his horse. The other two raced on, not pausing, and Fargo reined to a halt and heard the sound of hoofbeats moving away through the trees.

He stayed in place, waited, still listening, and his eyes peered into the box elder at the other side of the road. Nothing moved and the only sound was the hoofbeats fading away. He took the moment to reload as he felt the frown digging into his brow. It had been unlike any Indian attack he'd ever seen, almost inept, certainly without the reckless ferocity of most Indian attacks. Nothing about their actions had been in character, and his glance went to the arrows that littered the road. He bent down and picked up four of the shafts. Two held Ute markings and two were crudely made and unmarked. He stepped on and picked up three more. The first two held Ute markings on their shafts; the third was also unmarked.

Fargo's frown deepened as he stared down at the hoofprints in the soil. None were the unshod prints of Indian ponies, every mark made by a horseshoed hoof. His lips pulling back in a grimace, he strode forward to the motionless figure a half dozen yards away. The man wore only a loincloth and lay on his face, his long black hair falling in disarray over his head. Fargo's bullet had penetrated the base of his neck, and a line of red spilled down his back. As he peered down, Fargo saw that the man's skin alongside the blood had seemed to turn pale where the red liquid washed down his body. Fargo dropped to one knee, wet his finger with his lips, and ran it down the side of the man's torso. He lifted the finger to stare at the red-brown smudge on the tip.

"Dye," he murmured aloud, the reddish brown tone the probable product of crushed juniper berries and henna. He rose, used the top of his boot to turn the body over, and the long black hair fell from the man's head to lay on the ground beside him. His face had also been dyed, but his hair was close-cropped under where the wig had been. No Indians, none of them, Fargo muttered to himself as he returned to the Ovaro, and their strange actions had been explained. But nothing else, and as he climbed onto the saddle and the night descended, he began to put together what had happened.

Questions and answers pushed at each other. Why had they trailed him for days? There had to be only one answer. They weren't certain he was the one they wanted. They plainly knew that the man they wanted rode an Ovaro, and while Ovaros weren't commonplace, his wasn't the only one. They wanted to be sure and only when they saw him turn onto the old ox trail to Duchess were they certain he was the one they wanted. The Indian disguise was simple enough to explain. Someone wanted him to appear to have been killed by Indian arrows. There was always the chance that the attack might be seen, so the elaborate disguise was needed. Only, to their surprise, he had been ready for them. They were quick to break off the attack rather than have their masquerade exposed.

But the one attacker he'd brought down had done exactly that, and Fargo's thoughts continued to probe. Someone didn't want him to meet with Ellie Willis, and that someone knew Ellie had sent for him. Suddenly Ellie Willis was a very key figure, a source of all the questions that needed answers, and he put the Ovaro into a trot as the half moon rose. When he reached the town of Duchess, the half light revealed nothing special about it's double row of ramshackle houses with the main street running between them. The town saloon sent a square of light into the street when he passed, and he pulled to a halt some fifty yards on before a white clapboard, two-story building. Two lamps flanked the door and lighted a sign that read DUCHESS INN. He tethered the horse at the hitching post and strode into the building where a bald-headed man in shirtsleeves sat behind a front desk.

" 'Evening." The man nodded.

"You've an Ellie Willis registered here?" Fargo asked.

The clerk had no need to check his desk register, an indication that they weren't exactly chock-full with boarders. "Room four, end of hall on ground floor," he said.

Fargo nodded and found his way down the wide hallway to the last door. It was opened at his knock, and he felt a moment of surprise at the young woman who faced him, a round, pretty face with tightly curled blond hair and a wide mouth with full, sensuous lips. Ample breasts pushed out a dark green blouse, and a black cotton skirt folded itself around hips that curved nicely into long thighs. "Skye Fargo," he said, and she studied his face, a tiny furrow touching her smooth forehead.

"Your horse outside?" she asked and he nodded. She closed the door and strode down the hall and he followed. She stepped out of the inn and halted before the pinto, taking the horse in with a long glance. "All right," she said, turning to him. "Let's go back inside." Once again he followed her and she admitted him to the room, modest with a single bed and small dresser to one side. A stuffed chair and an end table completed the furnishings. "Can't be too careful," she said. "Besides, I wasn't sure you'd come." She paused and her eyes studied him again. "You seemed surprised when you saw me just now."

"Guess so," he admitted. "Somehow, I expected an older woman. You're much younger than I thought you'd be."

"Why'd you expect an older woman?" she asked.

"I'm not exactly sure of that. Maybe because Ben Adams is getting on, and you wrote that you were a friend of his," Fargo said.

"So you'd expect he'd have an older woman as a friend." Ellie Willis half smiled.

"More or less," Fargo admitted. "But then, the day's been full of surprises."

"Such as?" Ellie Willis asked.

"A passel of fake Indians tried to do me in," Fargo said.

"Fake Indians?" She frowned.

"That's right. I figure it has to be connected with whatever trouble Ben's got himself into," Fargo said. "Maybe you'd best start giving me the details on that."

"I can't, really," Ellie Willis said, and it was Fargo's turn to be surprised. She sat down on the edge of the bed and gave a small shrug of helplessness. "What I mean is that he never really told me anything."

"You just knew he was in trouble?" Fargo queried.

"Yes, by the way he was acting. But there's more. Whatever it is, or was, he's gone from it," she said.

Fargo felt irritation joining surprise inside him. "What's that mean?" He frowned.

"Ben took up and left," she said. "Two weeks ago."

"Just like that? No reasons? No explanations?"

"None. Didn't even say if he'd be back. It was too late for me to get hold of you, so I came to keep our meeting," Ellie Willis said and rose to stand before him. Her hand came up to rest against his chest, and her eyes were round and full of apology. "I'm sorry. There just was no way for me to reach you. I feel terrible about this."

"I'm not too happy about it, either, honey," Fargo admitted crossly, and then softened his words as she seemed sincerely contrite. "But I guess you're not to blame. As you said, it was too late to reach me."

Her hand tightened on his arm. "Thanks for understanding. You're as nice as Ben said you were.

But I feel it is my fault. If I hadn't gone and written you, you'd not have come all this way. I'd like to make it up to you," she said.

"Don't see how you could do that," Fargo said blandly.

"By finding out if something else Ben said about you was right," Ellie murmured.

"What was that?"

"He said you were quite a man with the ladies," she said, her full lips turning into a wide smile. "I'd like to find out. It would make me feel better about my bringing you all this way for nothing."

"Just that?"

"No, not just that. You're too damn good-looking to just let pass by," Ellie Willis said. "How's that for honesty?"

"Good enough," Fargo said. Her arms slid around his neck and her wide, sensuous lips found his. She pressed, opened her lips, and he felt her tongue darting out, drawing back, sliding out again, and the warm hunger of her was very real. He still had a lot of questions to ask, but they could wait. Pleasure before business. He always preferred that to the usual way, and he went with her as she fell back onto the bed.

His hands undid buttons and the dark green blouse came off, her camisole top slipping down, and he saw modest but very round breasts, surprisingly pale white with very dark red nipples and dark circles around each. He pulled off clothes as she slid from the skirt, and he saw wide hips, a little layer of extra flesh over them, a rounded belly and a modest little triangle that narrowed down to full thighs, also with an extra few pounds on them.

His hand encased one pale white breast, and it was very soft, flattening in at his touch. He put his mouth down to the dark red nipple and drew it in gently, and Ellie Willis gave a sharp cry of delight. "Yes, oh, Jeeez, yes," she said and pushed upward, and he took in more of the soft, pale white mound. She half turned, brought the other breast to him, and he took it, passing from one to the other as she cried out with each touch, and her hands moved slowly up and down his chest. Her tongue licked against the side of his face, and her sharp cries turned to eager moaning. When her hand reached down and touched his throbbing maleness, her body shuddered, drew back and thrust upward. "Oh, God, please, please," she murmured, and he saw her fleshy thighs falling open, twisting, closing, opening again.

He came to her, paused, then felt the moistness of her opened portal. He rested there for a moment, and she half screamed and pushed her torso upward at him, and he slid forward into the dark warm tunnel. "Oh, God, yes, yes . . . oh, oh yes," Ellie Willis moaned and moved with him, calling out with his very slow thrust. Her hands dug into his back, and her curved little belly jiggled as she pushed and lifted with her hips. Her thighs were clasped around him, pressing hard, squeezing as if in echo of his thrusts inside her. For all her eager delights, she managed to pace herself, and he drew in the wonderful pleasure of her wet warmth, soothing and exciting all at once, her very real wanting adding another dimension to their pleasure.

She had turned out in a completely unexpected way, but then the unexpected things were often the best. Her arms pulled his head down onto her soft breasts and held him there as her hips twisted and rose with him, and her gasps grew harsher. He felt himself gathering, spiraling, and suddenly her warm walls were contracting around him and a scream rose from her. She stiffened against him, suspended, embracing and embraced by that all-encompassing climax. He exploded with her and heard his own cry of ecstasy that was both release and despair, a forever moment. He sank down with her as she fell back onto the bed, but her thighs stayed around him, holding him inside her.

"Oh, God, oh God," Ellie Willis murmured, and his face pressed into her soft breasts, staying there and enjoying the touch of her, surrounding, enveloping. Finally her thighs fell open, and he slid from her to lay at her side. After a moment she turned to him, dark red nipples pressed against his chest. "That was something special," she said.

"I'm glad," he said.

"I feel better now, about everything," Ellie remarked.

"Good. I wouldn't want your conscience hurting on my account," Fargo said.

"It would have," she said.

"Where is Moon Lake?" he asked.

"About ten miles west."

"You and Ben live there?" he questioned.

"No, I lived in town. So did Ben. It's only a few miles from Moon Lake. They call it Moonside," Ellie told him.

"What did Ben do there?"

"He worked for a big rancher whose spread is near Moon Lake."

"And you?"

"I work in a store in town."

"What kind of a store?" Fargo asked.

She frowned at him and rose on one elbow. "Why all the questions?" she asked.

"I'm just naturally curious. You don't seem like the shopgirl type," Fargo said.

"Ladies wear," Ellie said and folded herself against him, her soft breasts flattening onto his chest. "Stay awhile, tomorrow and tomorrow night. I'd like that. I don't have to get back for another day."

"More conscience? Not that I could object to an offer like that," he added hastily.

"No, no more conscience. This is just for me. I haven't had a man in a long time, and I've never had one like you," she said. "Please?"

He shrugged. "I've nowhere to go except back," he said. She smiled and her wide mouth closed over his. Before she went to sleep in his arms she showed him again how appreciative she was. He slept contentedly late into the morning, and Ellie Willis woke as he did. He watched her use the washbasin. Her figure seemed more ample than it had during the night, little creases of extra flesh around her belly and thighs. But she definitely had an earthy sensuousness about her, and he was sorry to see her slip the brown dress on.

"I'll go out and wait for you. I understand they serve a good breakfast here," she said.

"All right. Then I've a horse to tend to," he told her.

"Let's spend the day doing nothing; we can look through town and relax together. I haven't had a day doing nothing in a long time," Ellie said wistfully.

"It's a deal," he said, and she hurried from the room. She was seated at a table in the dining room when he came out, biscuits and coffee waiting, and he realized he was hungry. She made small talk through breakfast and went with him when he took the Ovaro to the public stable and unsaddled the horse and pair for a roomy stall. Later she strolled through town with him, investigated the merchandise at the general store, and paused to read the schedule at the stage depot. "How'd you come here?" he asked.

"A friend drove me. She's coming to get me tomorrow," Ellie said as she strolled on with him, her arm linked in his, a sweet warmth to her. Outside of town they found a small stream and stretched out in the sun. "What will you do when you get back?" she asked.

"Find two or three jobs waiting for me. There usually are," he said. "You going to stay in Moonside and see if Ben comes back?"

"Yes," she said.

"Write me if he does. I'm just curious," Fargo said.

"If you like." She nodded and lay hard against him, and they watched the sun go down. When they returned to town, they ate in the dining room at the inn, corn fritters and chicken legs, and afterward, back in her room, she came to him with all the hungry wanting of the night before. The night grew deep before he slept, satiated with pleasant exhaustion. The trip hadn't turned out as he thought it would, he told himself, but it certainly hadn't been a waste of time. The pleasure of that thought added to the contentment of his deep sleep.

Once again, he indulged himself and slept into the morning and when he woke he felt for her warmth beside him. But his wandering hand found only empty air and he pulled his eyes open as he sat up. He was alone, in the room as well as the bed. Her clothes were gone, also, he saw. She must have very carefully slipped from the bed while he was still deep in sleep. She had to have been good for him not to have felt her leave. He rose, washed and strode from the room. The desk clerk looked up as he halted before him. "The young lady from room four, you see her this morning?" Fargo asked.

"Yes. She left," the clerk said. "Left a note for you." He handed Fargo a small square of paper and Fargo unfolded it to scan the few lines:

> It's best this way. I don't trust myself facing you come morning. Have a good trip back. . . . Ellie.

He frowned as he stuffed the note into his pocket and walked from the Inn. At the stable, he paid the night's bill, saddled the Ovaro and rode out of town. But the frown stayed on his brow. Suddenly something didn't fit. Or, perhaps more accurately, something new didn't fit. Suddenly Ellie's behavior seemed as strange as the fake Indians that had tried to kill him. A stab of uneasiness speared him and a new set of questions revolved through his mind.

He had believed her about Ben suddenly running off and how sorry she'd been for bringing him all this way for nothing. God knows she'd proved how contrite she'd been. With that kind of proof he'd no reason to disbelieve her. But now, her vanishing in the night simply didn't fit. It was plain that she had sent for him. Had somebody reversed her friendship and concern for Ben Adams? Had she really come to turn him around?

Something didn't set right at all and Fargo turned the Ovaro west. Ellie Willis had some more questions to answer.

LIFE ON THE FRONTIER

There's an epidemic with 27 million victims. And no visible symptoms.

It's an epidemic of people who can't read.

Believe it or not, 27 million Americans are functionally illiterate, about one adult in five.

The solution to this problem is you... when you join the fight against illiteracy. So call the Coalition for Literacy at toll-free **1-800-228-8813** and volunteer.

Volunteer Against Illiteracy.
The only degree you need is a degree of caring.